PEARSON

A FOUR FATHERS STORY

Mandy,

K WEBSTER

Mandy,

♡

Pearson (Four Fathers #3)

Copyright © 2018 K Webster

Cover Design: All By Design

Photo: Adobe Stock

Editor: Word Nerd Editing

Formatting: Raven Designs

I am selfish. Spoiled. A single father.

I do what I want because I can.
One of my four sons is dating the hot, young little neighbor...
Too bad it won't last long.
When I want something, I take it—even if it means taking from my son.

My name is Eric Pearson.

I am an unapologetic, egotistical, domineering man.
People may not like me, but it doesn't stop them from wanting me.

DEDICATION

To my husband, the ultimate alpha male.

WARNING:

You won't like this hero.

———PROLOGUE

ERIC

Two weeks earlier...

ALWAYS GET WHAT I WANT.

In business. In life. In the sack.

Always.

Most people don't get what they want because they ask for it, work toward it—they don't *take* it.

My entire life, that's exactly what I've done.

Take. Take. Take.

And it's worked beautifully. I'm the CEO of Four Fathers Freight, have four handsome sons who will make me proud one day, and more money than a man could dream of. Best of all, I have pussy on tap. If I want to get laid, all I have to do is smirk at the hottest woman in the room and within ten minutes, she'll be riding my cock like it's her birthright.

Taking has worked like a charm.

But there is one thing that I desperately want but haven't taken yet. She comes in a tiny, sexy little brunette package and belongs to a glowering asshole who lives next door—the daughter of a man I'd love nothing more than to *take* out.

She's also my seventeen-year old son's girlfriend.

So, while taking has always been my thing, for once in my selfish life, I don't take what I want. I sit back and watch her make out with my son, play grab ass with his brothers in our pool, and tease me every second of every goddamn day.

I don't take. I simply stare at what I'm not supposed to have.

But a man can only *take* so much before he loses control...

Especially a selfish bastard like myself.

ONE

ERIC

Present

"DUDE," TREVOR BLACKSTONE, MY BEST FRIEND since college mutters, "you're going to get your ass sent to prison or some shit."

I sip from my cold beer without sparing him a glance. My attention is on *her*. Always on her. Rowan Wheeler. Fuckin' jailbait...until tomorrow. My cock stirs, but I ignore it. It wouldn't be the first time I've gotten a boner in front of one of my best friends, or something I'd even give two shits about. But in front of all four of my sons and our sweet little neighbor? Isn't fucking happening.

"I'm just looking," I reply coolly.

He snorts. "You *look* like a damn tiger zeroing in on

his prey. What are you going to do? Maul her?"

The idea isn't bad.

Images of her sprawled out beneath me wearing my teeth marks does nothing to help the state of my semi-erect cock. "I can look."

"But you can't touch, Pearson," he reminds me, his voice turning slightly stern. Any other asshole I'd tell to fuck off, but Trevor is like the brother I never had. Hell, the kids even call him uncle.

"Right," I utter.

He grumbles, because we both know I'm going to touch. I'm going to touch so much, she'll never want the touch of anyone else again.

"Babe, grab me a Coke," my son Brock hollers.

My cold heart does a slight quiver in my chest. This is the biggest complication. Not the fact that she's seventeen for a few more hours. Not the fact that her father is a psycho asshole. Not the fact that she's probably a virgin I'd have to teach everything to. The biggest complication is him. My son. Brock Pearson.

He grins at her, boyish and goofy. Sure, he resembles me, probably the most of my four boys, but he's still a child. Only seventeen himself. The kid has his entire life ahead of him. Settling for the sexy-ass neighbor at such a young age is beneath him. Hell, when I went to college, I fucked more women than I care to remember. Being exclusive with Rowan will limit him. He won't get to experience things like his older brother Hayden has. Hayden, so much like myself, nearly got expelled for sleeping with one of his professors. If it weren't for my hefty donation to get him out of that heap of shit, he'd be living in my house feeling sorry for himself.

"Damn," Trevor mutters. He may be trying to protect Brock from getting hurt when his father no doubt bangs his girlfriend, but even he's not immune to Rowan's incredible beauty.

She reminds me of *her*.

A spike of irritation surges through me. Julia left us. Several years ago, at one of our annual backyard barbeques, after a humiliating meltdown where she accused me of being a cheating asshole in front of all our friends and family, she bolted. Packed a bag and never returned, leaving our four young sons to their ill-equipped father to finish raising. I haven't heard a word from the cunt since.

Julia was my one true love. I believed in all that bullshit at the time. Fell head over heels for her, married her as soon as I could, and knocked her up four times in a row. Life was bliss—until she called me out for having an affair.

"She looks like Julia," I mutter aloud.

Trevor grunts in agreement. "Another reason why you should stay the hell away."

Ignoring him, I watch as Rowan climbs out of the pool. Her dark brown hair is wet and hangs halfway down her back. With each step, her young ass bounces in the tiniest scrap of her bright orange bikini. She may be Brock's girlfriend, but every one of my boys is smitten with her. Hayden plays it cool, but I don't miss the way his eyes follow her everywhere. My fifteen and sixteen-year old sons, Camden and Nixon, get fucking boners they don't hide very well any time she's near.

She has that effect on people.

A sexy siren teasing every man with a working dick in the vicinity.

Hayden pretends like he's going to throw her back in the pool, but I know it's just an excuse to grab her. His arms wrap around her waist and she squeals. Brock, the blind idiot, doesn't even realize his older brother is rubbing his dick against her ass. But based on her blazing red cheeks, she now knows exactly how he feels about her.

"Asshole," she grumbles as she pushes him away. Her tits jiggle as she makes her way over to Trevor and me. The ice chest sits between our lounge chairs. I should tell her that her bikini top is askew and her pink nipple is showing, but I don't.

And Trevor, the dirty bastard, doesn't mention it either.

"Thirsty?" I question, my brow arched from behind

my sunglasses.

Her cheeks turn red again. "Brock is."

"Oh, I have no doubt about that," I say with a wolfish grin.

Understanding dawns in her brown eyes and her juicy plump pink lips part. "I...uh..."

My gaze is on her gorgeous tits as I reach into the ice chest and grab a can of Coke. When I hand it to her, our fingers touch, and she shivers.

"Thank you," she breathes. I skim my gaze over the long, silvery scar across her forehead. She's had it for as long as I've known her. Instead of marring her perfect features, it only accentuates how real she is. How gorgeous she is despite the scar that is her only flaw.

"My pleasure, angel."

Her smile is breathtaking and sweet. Someone like her would be so fun to mold into perfection in the bedroom. Whisper some flattering words in her ear. Teach her how to behave. Reward her when she does.

She turns and sways her curvy hips as she makes her

way back into the pool with my son. Trevor groans and digs around in the ice chest for another beer.

"She's hot," he mutters, "I'll give you that. She just seems more Levi's type."

Levi Kingston is an investor at Four Fathers Freight and part owner along with myself, Trevor, and our friend Mateo Bonilla. Trevor is the CFO and really good at what he does. Where Trevor and I have a friendship based on knowing each other for half our lives, Levi and I have a different sort of friendship.

We have similar dark, sexual preferences.

In fact, we frequent sex clubs and strip joints. He was the one to introduce me to hiring high-dollar prostitutes on our birthdays because, and I quote, "Good men deserve to be spoiled by bad women every now and again." He also sparked my interest in the whole daddy kink shit he's got a hard-on for.

And Rowan?

I would love to daddy the fuck out of her.

Bend her over my knee and spank her pretty little

ass.

My cock aches at the thought.

"He'll never touch her," I bite out, a little harshly.

Trevor laughs. "I'm just saying, he's into the young ones. You're usually into the expensive, high-maintenance chicks. The young and innocent ones are more his style."

"Maybe I'm bored and want something different," I challenge.

A sigh resounds from him. "You're going to fuck everything up, man."

"I haven't touched her yet."

"Yet," he utters. "You're fucking unbelievable."

Ignoring him, I rise from my lounger, peel off my T-shirt, and lose my sunglasses. I work hard on my physique. I may be forty-five, but I have the body of a much younger man. Countless hours in the gym each day ensure that. As I saunter over to the edge of the pool, I see both my younger boys smiling at me. A niggle of guilt sluices through me. I'm a shitty father. Sure, I provide, and provide well. All my boys drive expensive sports cars, wear the nicest clothes, and will go to the best colleges. They hurt for nothing.

Well, aside from my attention.

I'm not like most fathers.

I have a business to run—an empire to grow—so I may hand it over to them one day. I don't have time to play catch or watch movies or whatever the fuck most fathers do.

I give them money and that should be enough.

Nixon tosses a football at me, but instead of catching it, I let it soar past me. Trevor grabs it and tosses it back. Uncle Trevor, as they like to call him, fills that daddy role much better than I do. I let out a sigh of relief that he's wiped that puppy dog look off my son's face.

I make my way over to the diving board, catching Rowan's gaze along the way. I don't miss the way she rakes her curious eyes over my ripped chest. Smirking, I hop onto the diving board and walk to the edge. She's now standing in the middle of the pool. Alone. Like a heat-seeking missile, I dive into the cold water and swim beneath the surface to where I can see her. I move toward her, and the moment she's within reach, I grab her by the backs of the knees and pull her under. Her squeal makes my dick lurch in my trunks. She thrashes beneath the surface as she tries to escape me. I hear my sons hooting and hollering. We don't wrestle around much, but I figure this is what normal dads do. I can be normal for five minutes if it gives me an excuse to touch Rowan.

Someone strong tries to drag me away by my foot. I come up for air and see it's Camden. He's grinning like today's the best day of his life. I splash him, wriggle away, then seek her out again. Under the water, I see her retreating form swimming toward Brock. Once again, I grab her and pull her under. This time, our eyes meet under the water, and hers are wide with shock. She squirms from my grip, so I slide my hand up to get a better handle on her. My fingers slide under her suit and brush against the lips of her pussy. Her thrashing stops. I pretend as though I don't know where I have my hand and push my longest finger against her cunt. I'm met with tight resistance, but my finger breaches her opening to my first knuckle.

Bubbles shoot from her mouth as she gets pulled away from my grasp. I resurface to see Brock kissing her neck.

"I saved you," he says, his voice playful.

Camden tries to tackle me from behind, and I easily toss him into the deep end. Nixon and Trevor are having a heated football tossing match while Hayden watches me with a death glare from the other side of the pool. I wink at my oldest son.

When I return my stare to Rowan, she's blinking innocently, as if I didn't just have my finger inside her. Her throat is bright red, and she seems distracted as Brock kisses the side of her neck.

I swim a few laps and eventually grow bored.

One day, I'm going to have that girl.

Soon. Really fucking soon.

TWO

R O W A N

I STARE OUT MY WINDOW AND RIGHT INTO BROCK'S. His curtains are open, but he's not home yet. I'm eager to hang out with him before Daddy gets home tonight. Things are getting more serious lately.

Well...they were.

Shame ripples through me as I remember how turned on I was yesterday watching Brock's father lying on the pool lounger, drinking his beer. He's like the older, sexier, more muscled version of my boyfriend. I'd been drooling over him all afternoon. And when he swam straight for me, I'd been thrilled. His eyes are always on me, but he never acts on the heat burning in his steel-blue gaze. Not that he'd want someone like me. Little Rowan Wheeler, the virgin neighbor who's still a daddy's girl.

I've seen the women Eric brings home. Tall, leggy, gorgeous, fake. He loves them dripping in shiny jewelry and wearing very little clothes. In comparison, I'm nothing. It's strange to me that he seems to always be staring my way. Could someone like him want to be with someone like me?

The thought brings guilt. My boyfriend is Brock. We haven't had sex yet, but I know it's coming. We're working up to it. Today, I plan on giving him his first blow job. Well, I hope it's his first. He told me it was. It's certainly my first blow job. It may be my birthday, but I want to give this to him.

It will erase some of the guilt.

Remind me I'm with Brock and not Eric.

Still, I can't help but think about the shock of having his finger inside me. I think it was an accident, but his gaze was positively wolfish. Promising. Like he wanted to do more when people weren't around. Thankfully, he never got the chance. Brock walked me home, and I didn't see any more of Eric Pearson.

I abandon the window on a hunt for something sexy to wear. If I'm going to give my first blow job, I want to look hot doing it. I peel off my T-shirt and rummage around in my closet for something that will hug my curves. I settle for a white halter-top dress. Once I yank it from the hanger, I walk out of the closet and toss it on the bed. I pull off my bra since it doesn't go with the dress and stand in the middle of my room in nothing but my lacy pink panties.

My core throbs, and I wonder if Brock will go down on me again. Last weekend, when his dad was away on a trip with his friend and my dad was on business, I stayed over. Brock and I slept naked together. We didn't have sex, but we got close. He licked at my clit until I almost came. I was on the edge and hadn't quite leapt off when Hayden busted us.

More shame burns through me.

Last summer, before Hayden went off to college, we all got really drunk on Eric's liquor. Hayden pulled me onto his lap once his brothers passed out and kissed me dizzy. We made out for hours. I was silly enough to think he'd ask me out or something, but the next day, he acted like nothing happened. Not long after that, he went to college and I started dating Brock.

Thoughts of all the Pearson men have me feeling flushed. Absently, I reach down and run my fingers over my clit through my panties. It feels good. I imagine it's Brock's fingers, but my fantasy turns dirty quickly. Brock morphs into Eric. Soft touches become rough ones. Sweet words become biting ones.

"Mmmm," I whimper.

Steel-blue eyes pinning me. A hard, stone-like body pressed against my chest. Full lips kissing mine.

My orgasm is close, but still so far away. With a frustrated groan, I give up and throw on my dress. Once it's knotted behind my neck, I look at my reflection. I can't say I'm displeased. According to my dad, I look just like my mother. I never knew her since she died having me. She had silky brown hair like mine and chocolate-colored eyes. I haven't seen many pictures because it upsets him to keep them out, but I know I have her pouty lips too.

I hear the door open and close downstairs. My hopes of seeing Brock are dashed knowing my father is here. Since it's my birthday, he'll want to take me to dinner or something. With a huff, I push my dark brown hair behind my ears and look around my room. When my eyes land on Daddy's newest gift, I suppress a shudder.

I'm eighteen, not eight.

Of course I told him I loved it, but secretly, I'd been horrified. Daddy built me a dollhouse. It's chest high and made from real wood. On one side, it looks exactly like the front of our house, even down to the gray shutters. On the other side, it's open and gives a bird's eye view into an exact replica of our house. Even the Barbie's room is pink like mine. Frilly and pink and over the top. I don't have the heart to tell him I'll be going to college in a few short months. I'll live in a dorm and trade in all this girly shit for the college life.

But he's been both parents to me. He's a cool dad

and gives me freedom. However, he's still a parent in the sense that he makes me eat right and makes sure I'm taking care of myself. School is important to him and my grades can't be anything less than stellar.

"My little girl is growing up," he says from my doorway, pride in his voice.

I turn to look at my dad. Jax Wheeler. He's not much older than Eric and has a similar physique. I'd always thought men were supposed to get flabby and gross with age, yet all the men I know have only gotten better. It makes me hope my dad will find him a nice woman to settle down with. He's always so lonely, and it breaks my heart. Seeing that he owns a pharmaceutical company and runs every day at five in the morning to keep in shape, he should have women falling at his feet. I seriously don't get it.

"Hey," I say with a smile.

He walks into the room, opens his arms for a hug, and I walk into his embrace. When I start to pull away, I notice a drop of blood on his shirt.

"Did you hurt yourself?" I ask, pointing to the spot.

His smile falls as he inspects it. "Yeah, shaving."

I open my mouth to ask him where the cut is when he gives me a sheepish smile.

"Rowan, how mad at me would you be if I rescheduled your birthday dinner?"

At this, I laugh. "Depends on the reason."

He rubs at the back of his neck and shrugs. "I met this woman recently..."

"You have a date!" I screech, a huge smile on my face.

"Something like that." He smirks at me.

"Go!" I say with a giggle. "And take a shower. You stink."

He chuckles. "I promise I'll make it up to you."

"I know you will."

His gaze flits over to the dollhouse, and he beams with pride. Just another reason why I'd never say a thing about it. It's not his fault that he doesn't know how to raise a girl. He's tried his best, and I love him for that.

While Daddy gets ready, I wait impatiently by the

window. Brock finally comes home, waving at me from his window, and I wave back. The moment my father leaves, I all but run next door.

Nixon answers immediately after I knock. He may only be sixteen, but he's just as tall and buff as Brock. Unlike his older brothers, he's yet to develop the sexy smirk they seem to share with their father. I stand on my toes to ruffle his hair, then bounce through the house on a mission to find Brock. Once inside his room, I shut the door and begin tugging at the knot on my dress. Brock's hungry gaze roves over me as the dress falls to the floor beside the bed.

"Wow," he says in awe. "So pretty."

I smile as I do my best to walk seductively toward him. Based on the way his cock tents his basketball shorts, I'd say he's definitely aroused. He sits up and hangs his legs off the side of the bed and I come to stand between them.

"Happy birthday," he says with a panty-melting grin.

I lean forward and kiss his mouth. "What did you get me?"

Panic flashes in his eyes. Quickly, he schools it away. "I got you me."

I laugh until I realize he's not joking. "Oh." Tears prick my eyes, but I blink them back and smile at him.

"You could ride my cock," he offers, his gaze hooded.

A pang of nervousness flits through me. Suddenly, I don't feel so ready for sex. Distracting him, I fall to my knees and rub his dick through his shorts. "I could suck your cock instead."

"Fuck yes," he grunts, lifting his hips to assist me in pulling his shorts off. I slide them down his thighs and grip his dick in my hand.

"I'm not sure what to do," I whisper.

He strokes my hair and smiles. "Put your lips on it. Maybe use your tongue. You'll figure it out."

I swallow down my unease. My thoughts keep going to this summer. He'll turn eighteen too, but he always gives me the runaround when I talk about college. It's almost as if...

He wouldn't break up with me, would he?

"Do you think our dorms will be close?" I ask, my tongue teasing his salty tip.

A hiss escapes him, but he avoids my stare. "Maybe."

Frowning, I sit back slightly. "Brock, what's going to happen to us?"

Anger flashes in his eyes and his jaw clenches. "Are we seriously discussing this with my dick in your mouth?"

His tone stings me. My instinct is to crawl away and grab for my dress. I'm about to when there's a knock. Before I can move, his bedroom door swings open and someone growls. Like an animal. And holy hell, does it drop a match and set my soul on fire.

THREE —————

E R I C

MY TEMPER FLARES WHEN I SEE AN ALMOST NAKED Rowan on her knees in front of my son with his dick in her hand. A possessive need to pluck her up and spank her tiny little ass is overwhelming. I fist both hands as I step into the room.

"What the fuck is going on here?" I snarl.

She screeches and scrambles to her feet, her arms crossing over her chest. As if her skinny arms could hide her bouncy tits. It just makes them look fatter and juicier. I'm going to bruise the hell out of them. Soon.

"Dad," Brock says, his voice hoarse as he quickly gets decent.

"This," I seethe, "is not going to happen under my roof."

Rowan's big brown eyes well with tears and she glances at her dress smashed beneath my black leather Gucci dress shoe.

"You're both going to college soon," I snap. "It's in your best interest to break up and make things at the end of the summer less painful."

"Dad, stop," Brock snaps as he rises from the bed.

I hold my hand up to him and shake my head. "Your car..." I trail off, pinning him with a hard stare that intimidates most men I do business with. "I can make it go bye-bye." I make a waving motion to drive home my point.

His gaze darkens and jaw clenches. I bought him an Audi A7 as an early graduation present. Sleek black. All leather interior. It set me back about seventy grand. He knows what a lucky little shit he is to have such an expensive vehicle.

"You're breaking up with me?" Rowan asks, her swollen bottom lip trembling.

Brock winces, but doesn't have the balls to follow

through. Good thing for him, I've got balls made of motherfucking titanium.

"Go to my office," I boom. "You're still a minor, son, which means this shit between you two is pretty goddamn serious." I turn and pin her with an icy glare. "You could get arrested, angel."

A teary, choked sound escapes her. Brock huffs, but he knows I've won this round. He mutters out a soft apology to Rowan before rushing from the room. Once he's gone, I stare her down. Tears streak down her red cheeks. She looks positively devastated.

Exactly how I want her.

Pulling out my phone, I take a picture of her looking like a beautiful mess. For my own personal stash. The beginning of many. Her eyes widen.

"For evidence," I say with a smirk.

At this, she sobs quietly.

"You're eighteen, little girl," I bite out. "That means what you were doing was a fast track to statutory rape."

"Rape?" she murmurs, horror in her tone.

"He's a minor, and now I have evidence. Shall I call the cops? What would your daddy think about that?"

Her shoulders hunch as she cries. Fuck, she's so damn pretty. Those quivering lips were made for my cock.

"Please don't call the cops," she murmurs.

I soften my gaze. "I suppose I could change my mind."

Her features light up with hope. "Really?"

"As long as you are punished accordingly."

She lets out a breath and her face falls. "Oh."

"It's nothing you can't handle," I say in a low voice.

Her brown eyes shine with curiosity. "I should be punished."

"You should," I agree. I walk over to the bedroom door and close it. "Put your hands on the door."

She blinks at me several times in shock. "Why?"

A surge of anger ripples through me at her questioning me. "Because I fucking said so."

Her body jolts at my harsh words, and she walks toward me, her arms still crossed over her luscious tits. She glances at me, searching for something. I give her a small smile of encouragement. This relaxes her considerably. She slowly moves her arms to press her palms to the door. Her back is to me, and my dick is stone in my slacks knowing her tits are bare.

"When my boys misbehave," I growl as I unbuckle my belt and yank it from the loops with a loud swoosh, "I whip them."

A whimper of fear escapes her and her body shakes. She turns to look at me over her shoulder, her brown eyes wide with terror. Folding my snakeskin belt in half, I softly run it across her ass over her panties, and her sobs grow louder.

I lean into her, pressing my aching erection against her hip. My mouth finds her ear over her hair.

"I have to punish you so you'll learn you can't do such awful things, angel. You understand that, right? This will hurt me a lot more than it hurts you." My voice is gentle. She doesn't need to know I'll enjoy the fuck out of her screams.

"R-Really?" She sniffles and tilts her head to the side

as though she wants my mouth on her neck.

Later.

When she's been a good girl.

"Oh, yes," I croon. "I'd much rather reward you."

"I want to be rewarded."

"By me?"

"Yes," she breathes.

"You liked my finger inside your tight pussy yesterday," I state.

She whines.

"Correct, angel?"

Another whine.

"Little girls who want to play with men need to use their mouths." I nip at her ear. "I really want you to use your mouth."

"Y-Yes. I liked it."

"Why?"

"Because I want to be touched."

"By Hayden?" I tease.

"What?" she mutters. "No."

"By any of my boys?"

She doesn't answer right away, then gives me what I'm looking for. "No."

"Who do you want to touch you?"

"You."

"What a good little girl you are," I praise. "I'm going to punish you, and then I'm going to make it all better." I wrap my arm around her front and pinch her nipple slightly. The gasp that trembles from her is one of shock. "Is that what you want?"

"Yes."

"Did you give your cunt up to my son?"

"N-No."

"You really are a good girl," I mutter. Releasing her, I step away and admire her tight ass. It jiggles each time she shivers in anticipation. Her lacy panties make my dick really fucking hard.

"Push your panties down your thighs to your knees and spread your legs slightly."

"Mr. Pearson," she whispers.

"Eric." A beat. "Say my name."

"Eric."

"Do as I say, angel. Please don't make me repeat myself."

She removes her hands from the wall and spreads her legs, then pushes her panties down. The first thing I notice is they're wet. She's soaked. Deep down, she's a naughty girl.

"You've ruined your panties," I snap, scaring her and making her yelp. I palm her bare ass. "I love it."

Her tense body relaxes, and she tentatively places her palms back on the door.

"This is going to hurt, angel. Your ass is going to bleed before I'm done with you." I run the belt over her skin again. "Does your daddy whip you?"

"No," she chokes out.

"Because he's not your real daddy." I let my words hang thick in the air. She doesn't argue. Good fucking girl.

"Ready?" I ask.

She nods.

"How many times should I whip you?"

"Umm..." she trails off. "Ten?"

I chuckle. My sweet little masochist. "Oh, angel, you can't handle ten whippings. You'd pass out. How about half that? Five sound good?"

"Yes."

"Yes, what?"

"Uh, Eric."

"No."

"Sir?"

"Daddy," I snap. It makes me smile knowing her stupid-ass father would blow a fucking gasket if he was aware of what I was doing to his precious baby girl.

"What?"

"Fucking say it if you want me to spank your pretty ass."

"But..."

"No buts, angel. Either you want it, or you don't want—"

"Okay, Daddy."

I smirk. One of these days, I'll get her on film worshipping my cock. You never know when you might need ammo against your sworn enemy. I'm sure her real daddy would love to get a video of his bad little girl calling another man by his name.

Without warning, I rear my arm back and strike with my belt, hitting her every bit as hard as I would my sons. Her scream is a silent one. Horrified. Filled with terror. Shocked.

I get in another whip before she gets ahold of her senses and tries to run from me. She ducks around me, darting for the bed, her panties falling to her ankles. They become entangled, but before she falls, I pounce on her and push her to the bed.

Whap! Whap!

She wails and thrashes, but I'm not done. I fist her hair and force her head down as I deliver the last blow. As soon as I'm done, I toss the belt away and sit beside her. She's sobbing so hard, I worry she'll vomit—and I don't do fucking vomit. Yanking her to me, I pull her into my lap, crushing her to my chest. At first, she's stiff, but then she clings to the front of my dress shirt as she cries. I stroke her hair gently. My cock is painfully hard. I'd love nothing more than to stick my cock in her virgin hole, but if I want her eating out of my palm, this is what she needs first.

I hold her for a long while until her crying subsides. Her soft breathing indicates she cried herself to sleep. So damn cute. I kiss the top of her head before sliding my palm to her ass. She winces and lets out a pained moan. When I inspect my fingertips, I don't see blood. One day soon, she'll fuck up bad enough that I'll have to draw blood. Until then, a red and bruised ass will have to do.

"Angel?"

"Yeah?"

"Are you okay?

She nods, but won't look at me. I want to see her sad eyes.

"Words. Use them. I want to see your pretty eyes

too."

Her body shifts until she's looking up at me. I cup her cheek. When I run my thumb along her jaw, her eyes flutter closed. So damn impressionable. This girl will do anything for me. One day. I just need to train her properly. Thanks to Levi and his sexual quirks, I've learned a few things over the past year or so.

"Tomorrow, I'm going to hurt you."

She blinks at me, terror in her eyes. "What?"

"With my cock," I say in a teasing tone.

Her smile is sexy. "I want that."

"You and Brock are over," I remind her, my nostrils flaring.

"Okay."

"I want you to sit on my lap and spread your legs with your back against my chest," I instruct. My cock strains against my boxers. Not today, big boy.

Obeying like a good girl, she twists until she's sitting with her feet resting on the bed on either side of my outer thighs. I wish I could see her cunt, open and inviting, but I can be patient. I've waited this long for her...what's another day?

Sliding my hand around her, I caress her tight stomach, then slip it south toward her pussy. She lets out a sharp gasp when my fingertip slides down her slit, rubbing over her clit along the way.

"You like that?" I murmur against her hair.

"Yes," she breathes.

"Yes, what?"

She's quiet for a moment, then whispers, "Daddy."

I pull my hand from her cunt and point to her bedroom. "What would your real daddy do if he saw this?"

"He'd kill you," she says without hesitation.

I laugh. He could fucking try. "Okay, angel. It's a good thing he's not home, huh?"

She nods, and I bring my hand back to her bare pussy. I'm not sure if she shaves or waxes, but it's smooth and silkier than any cunt I've been in contact with in the past ten years. I've never been into younger women. Just

Rowan. She's different. I want to possess every part of her.

As I massage her slowly, I tease her with questions. "Are you on the pill, Rowan?"

"No."

"I'm going to come all inside your cunt tomorrow. So many times. It's going to run down your legs and make a big fucking mess."

She tenses.

"I'm going to get you pregnant."

My finger slides into her soaked opening. She softly whimpers my name as I gently fingerfuck her.

"You want me to knock you up and piss your daddy off?"

"No," she says, mild irritation in her tone.

I push another finger into her, not as gently, enjoying the way she squirms. "Wrong answer. Tell me what I want to hear."

"Eric," she pleads, her pussy clenching hard around my two fingers. This cunt is going to squeeze the fuck out of my cock.

"Words," I snap.

"Okay, yes."

"Yes, what?"

"Daddy," she murmurs, shame in her voice.

"You just turned eighteen and you want your forty-five-year-old neighbor to put a baby inside your teenage body? Is that what I'm hearing?"

"Why are you doing this?"

"Goddammit, angel, answer the fucking question," I seethe. I rub my thumb on her clit to help her say the words that need to be said.

"Yes, I want that. I want you to be careless and fuck a baby into me."

I grin against her hair. "You're dirty."

She moans as I increase the pressure on her clit. I want to put another finger inside her juicy cunt, but she might not be able to take it. As she nears her orgasm, based on her breathing and shaking, I decide to do it anyway. It'll be one less thing to have to deal with later.

I push the third finger in past the other two, ignoring her squirms and screams. I fuck her hard with my hand as though it's my cock, reveling in the way I destroy her innocence. She cries at the pain, but then my thumb expertly strokes her clit. The sweet girl is helpless against my attack.

"Give in, angel," I whisper softly.

She jolts and her back arches as the orgasm strikes. It's beautiful to watch and hear as she shudders like I'm performing an exorcism on her. Eventually, she comes down from her high. I slide my fingers back out and smear her essence all over her stomach.

"Tomorrow, I'm going to see what you taste like." I give her pussy a playful swat. "Time to go home. Your punishment is over, and I want you rested for tomorrow. Don't worry, I was only teasing you earlier. You'll get on the pill and we'll be careful. The last thing I need is any more goddamn kids." Grabbing her narrow waist, I hoist her up and plop her down beside me. I rise from the bed and locate her panties. When I turn to look at her, she has her bottom lip captured between her teeth and her rosy cheeks are still tearstained.

"You're beautiful," I tell her with a smile.

The girl melts at my praise. It makes my dick hard at how easy she is to mold to my liking. I drop to one knee and use her panties to clean up the mess on her stomach.

"Spread your legs and let me see the damage," I utter lowly.

Shyly, she spreads her thighs, and I admire her wet, red pussy. Her lips are swollen with a smear of sticky blood mixed with her arousal. I dab at it with her panties, soiling the lacy fabric.

"All clean," I say with a wide grin. "I'm going to keep these."

She nods as I stand and tuck the panties into my pocket. I walk over to her dress and pick it up from the floor. After I shake it to get the wrinkles out, I make my way back over to her.

"Up," I order.

She shakily stands. As though she's a little girl, I help

her step into her dress, then pull it up over her creamy curves.

"Lift your hair."

Her arms raise as she collects her silky tresses. I tie the knot behind her neck, then motion for her to release her hair. It falls down and she eyes me with uncertainty.

Capturing her jaw in my firm grip, I tilt her head up so I can stare into her pretty eyes. "Happy birthday, Rowan."

Her lips tug into a smile I want to suck right off her face. Leaning forward, I brush my lips across hers and kiss her softly on the mouth. A sweet, needy moan escapes her, and she parts her lips, inviting me for more. Because she's been such a good, compliant girl, I give her a reward. I kiss her deeply. A kiss that's meant to stake a claim. She's mine—she'll soon learn that. Her tongue is eager against mine, and she kisses me back as though she accepts my possessive unspoken proclamation. I suck on her tongue, then nibble at her bottom lip before pulling away.

"Come to my office. I have your present in there."

Her brows scrunch together. "My present?"

"It's your birthday. Of course I got you a present."

Crimson red paints her high cheekbones. "Oh."

With a smile, I stroke my fingers through her soft hair. Her eyes flutter closed, and she leans into my kind gesture.

"Rowan?"

"Yes?"

"Who do you belong to?"

"You."

I wink at her before grabbing her wrist. "Don't ever forget it."

FOUR

R O W A N

Oh. My. God.

What just happened?

My mind is reeling. My body aches and burns. My heart is pounding in my chest.

In a matter of thirty minutes, I went from Brock's girlfriend to...Eric's angel? I'm having trouble processing this. His hand is firm and hot wrapped tightly around my wrist. It's possessive and claiming as he marches me out of Brock's room without shame.

I, on the other hand, can't lift my head.

Their eyes.

I feel all their eyes on me.

They had to have heard my screams, yet none dared to enter the room. On one hand, I'm glad, but I'm also irrationally angry at them. All four boys. I thought they cared about me. I could have been getting hurt. I was getting hurt. By their father. And none of them tried to stop it.

Of course, they didn't know I enjoyed every second of it.

The whipping hurt. The way he talked to me hurt. The way he fingerfucked me hurt.

But I liked it.

Something's wrong with me.

Am I so desperate to be grown and out from under Daddy's overprotective thumb that I'm rebelling?

Eric stops, and I peek up beneath my lashes to face the boys who didn't intervene. The worried stare of Camden, the youngest. The impassive, unreadable expression on Nixon's face. And the furious, hateful glare of Hayden.

"Great news, boys," Eric says cheerfully. "Rowan isn't going to jail."

"What the fuck, Dad?" Hayden hisses.

I don't say a word and turn my attention back to my feet.

"I'm going to give her the birthday present I have for her, then I want one of you boys to walk her home so she gets there safely," Eric rumbles, authority dripping from his tone. He owns us all in some way. With his kids, he dangles money over their heads, and if they screw up, they don't get it. With me?

I'm not sure why I'm under his spell, but I so am.

He had me the moment he walked into Brock's room and shut the door, enclosing us in together. I allowed him to do all those things to me. I liked them. *Oh God.*

"I'll walk her," Hayden bites out. "I'll be on the front porch."

Eric squeezes my wrist and guides me down the hallway. Like a gentleman, he releases my hand and offers me his elbow. I grab hold of it and we walk side by side down the fancy staircase. It makes me feel like royalty.

We make it into the foyer and he escorts me to his office, where I find Brock sitting in a chair, staring up at the ceiling. After he gave me up so easily, I'm having a hard time looking at him.

"Rowan," he utters.

I ignore him and squeeze Eric's arm. He reaches over and pats my hand in support.

"Son," he says to Brock. "I want you to see how a man treats a woman. One day, when you're grown, you'll need to know these things."

Brock starts to speak, but Eric shakes his head at him.

"Don't talk. Listen. She's not yours anymore. All she is to you is a lesson," Eric explains, then turns to me and smiles. "Ready for your present?"

"You got her a present?" Brock asks in confusion.

Eric grits his teeth and glares at his son. "A real man gets his woman a present on her birthday."

My heart swells. His woman? I'm his woman?

"She's not your—" Brock starts, but Eric interrupts.

"Shut your goddamn mouth and listen!" His nostrils flare with fury. Eric is strong and powerful. Authority seems to pulsate the air around him. It's easy to get intoxicated by it. Brock, apparently afraid of his father, cowers and wisely zips his lips.

"On your knees, angel." Eric smiles at me.

I blink in confusion. When his jaw ticks, my heart rate quickens. I don't want to upset him. Quickly, I drop to my knees and rest my butt on my heels. My sex hurts from his violation, but it's a reminder that he's staked his claim. He reaches into his desk drawer and pulls out a Tiffany box wrapped in a thick white silky ribbon.

"For you," he says, his voice husky and deep.

I shiver and take the gift. My knees hurt at the wood digging into my bony flesh, but I ignore it as I tug the ribbon away, letting it fall to the floor in front of me. When I open the box, I find a silver choker necklace inside with a large silver heart encrusted in diamonds hanging from the center.

It's beautiful.

"A fucking dog collar?" Brock mutters, his voice shaking in horror.

I tense at his words. It's too pretty to be a dog collar.

Eric ignores him as he pulls the necklace from the box and flips the heart around to show me the inscription.

Daddy's girl.

My mouth pops open, knowing it's referring to him and not my real dad. That means...he planned this.

"I was always coming for you," he murmurs, his other hand reaching forward to stroke his fingers through my hair. He sits in his desk chair and pats his knee. "Come closer."

I crawl on my knees until I'm between his parted thighs.

"Hair, angel."

Beaming at his sweet endearment, I lift my hair. He fastens the necklace, then motions for me to release my hair.

"Isn't she beautiful?" he says to Brock.

Brock grumbles, and Eric once again ignores him as though his opinion doesn't matter anyway.

"Stand," he orders.

I rise to my feet in front of him.

"Rowan," Brock says, his voice weak, "you don't have to do this."

A burst of anger surges up inside me like a gasoline tsunami. I jerk my head his way and hiss, "Mind your own fucking business."

Brock gapes at me. Staring at him, it makes me realize how young he looks. He doesn't have the dark five o'clock shadow like his father. He doesn't have the crow's feet at the corners of his eyes or the slight bit of grey at his temples.

He's a boy.

Turning, I smile at Eric.

My man.

"Thank you, Eric." I beam at him so hard, my cheeks hurt. "I love it."

"Don't ever take it off," Eric says, his voice turning cold. It makes me shiver.

"I won't," I rush out, wanting to appease him.

His handsome face breaks into a boyish grin that makes me want to rub my thighs together. "Good girl.

You learn quickly." He takes my hand and kisses the back of it. "Go home. We'll continue this tomorrow."

He releases me, and I know I'm dismissed. With a soft sigh, I walk way. Before I reach the door, Brock spits out, "So, it's like that, huh? We break up and you bone my dad? Are you fucking kidding me? I always knew you were a wh—"

"Finish that fucking statement and I'll make sure your life is a living hell," Eric roars, rising to his feet. His chest heaves, his fury nearly knocking me over.

Brock shrinks in his seat, avoiding eye contact with me.

"Goodnight, beautiful." Eric is once again all smiles.

I wave to him before darting out the door. The necklace is heavy, but I know it must have cost a fortune. My lips curve into a smile as I all but bounce through the foyer. As soon as I reach the front door, I let a small giggle escape.

This is unreal.

I'm seriously with *the* Eric Pearson.

He's rich and powerful and hot.

Not his sons.

Him.

"What did he do to you?" an angry voice demands the moment I step onto the front porch.

Hayden leans against a pillar, a cigarette between his teeth. His scowl is fierce, and he puffs on his cancer stick as though he's trying to punish it.

"What?"

He glowers at me. "Don't fucking play dumb, Rowan."

I wince at his tone. "Nothing."

"Nothing?" he demands as he flicks the cigarette to the ground and stomps on it. "Your screams sure as fuck didn't sound like nothing." He stalks over to me until he's towering above me.

Holding my ground, I lift my chin and face off with him. "If it sounded like something more than nothing, maybe you should have done something about it."

His eyes narrow. "What. Did. He. Do?"

I shove his hard chest, but he doesn't budge. "None

of your business!"

He grabs my wrists when I move to shove him again. "Did he rape you?"

"What?" I hiss. "Are you serious?"

"Tell me. I'll kill that bastard if he hurt you."

Jerking my hands from his grip, I turn on my heel and run through the yard toward my house, his heavy footsteps thudding behind me. I almost make it up my porch steps and into my house before he has his arm wrapped around my waist. He twists me around and pushes me up against my front door.

"I'll kill him," he murmurs before he tries to kiss me.

Fury, once again, explodes from within me. Like a cat straight from hell, I rake my claws across his face. He hisses in shock and stumbles away.

"Do not ever touch me again," I seethe.

His anger is gone, and he flashes me a wounded expression. *You lost your chance, buddy.* When he starts for me again, I hiss, "Don't come near me."

"Rowan." His voice is choked and pained, like he's

upset.

I'm upset.

How dare he?

"Leave. I'm home. Safe. Now, leave before I call your father." I smirk at him.

His gaze darkens. "He's going to ruin you, babe. He ruins everything he touches."

My ass still burns, and I know I'll be sporting some bruises. I feel as though I've been raped by a baseball bat. Everything hurts, aches, or burns, yet I've never felt so cared for.

"Maybe I want to be ruined." With a sassy wave, I turn on my heel and go inside. It isn't until I'm soaking in a hot bath and touching my new necklace that I take a moment to let it all sink in.

This was the best birthday of my life.

FIVE ——————

E R I C

"**N**OPE. NEXT," I GRUMBLE, LOOKING AT MY ROLEX for the eighteenth time in the past twenty minutes.

Levi sits up in his chair and raises a brow at me. "What crawled up your ass and died?"

My jaw clenches. "I have something I need to get to and this shit is a waste of time."

Levi, the bastard, laughs. "Well, too fucking bad. You're going to hear this shit out and then you can go run to your high-dollar whore."

Mateo smirks, and I pin him with an icy stare.

"So, you two assholes are tag-teaming me now?" I snap, then turn to glare at Trevor. "You too?"

Trevor holds his hands up in mock surrender. "I

didn't say a word."

"Who's the lucky girl?" Mateo probes. "Last time you acted like this big of a dick was when you started seeing Julia."

Nosy bastard. I push back, because that's the kind of motherfucker I am. "How's Karelma?" I lick my lips. His daughter is eighteen and has quite the ass on her. I've often thought about tapping that ass just to piss him off.

He scowls, his features growing stormy. "I sent her away. Ever since Valencia died, she's been acting out."

"Anyway," Levi growls, slinging a folder my way. "They're every bit as profitable as DSL. They're up and coming. We buy now at this price, and we take that territory and market share."

Unimpressed, I flip open the file. The numbers are fine, but Trevor will make a better assessment. I shove them over to him. He takes the file and leans back in his chair, resting his ankle on his knee, a half smile on his face.

I check my watch again, which has Mateo and Levi both laughing at me. Fucking pricks. I just want to get home. Yesterday afternoon was just the tip of the iceberg. Tonight, I'm going to defile Rowan Wheeler.

"What's the deal with Jax Wheeler?" Trevor asks out of the goddamn blue.

I snap my glare his way. He's no longer looking at the folder, but instead has a worried expression on his face. Does he think I'll run into trouble with that asshole? Nobody fucks with me. Jax Wheeler will learn that the hard way. I'm going to ruin his daughter's sweet cunt and there's not a damn thing he can do to stop me.

"It's not about Rowan," Trevor groans. "It's about Lucy."

"Who the fuck is Lucy?" Levi demands.

Trevor's normally playful disposition is replaced by one of worry. "She's my...never mind. I just want to know what Jax's deal is. I thought he was a pharmaceutical rep."

"Yeah? So?" I'm already bored of this conversation. I'd much rather discuss how Jax's daughter is going to squeal like a pig soon. I check my watch. Again.

"He's got money, obviously. The dude lives next door

to your preppy ass. And he's got a grown daughter. So why the hell is he over at the middle school all the time?" Trevor asks, his brows furrowed.

I shrug. "Does it look like I'm Jax's keeper?"

"Nope," Levi says with a grin. "But maybe you should learn his schedule if you're going to fuck his little girl."

Mateo sits up and frowns. "What?"

"I'm done with you assholes," I snap and rise. "If Trevor says this shit is good, then go ahead with it. You dicks can finish this meeting on your own. Some of us would like to get laid this century."

Stalking out of the boardroom, I make a pass to my office to make sure I lock up. I pass by Levi's office and movement makes me pause. When I peek in the window, I see our office assistant, Kristyn Marshall, sitting at his desk. Curiosity has me pushing open his door and sticking my head inside.

"Can I help you?" I ask.

Her cheeks blaze crimson and she shakes her head. "No, sir." I rake my gaze over her tits spilling out of the top of her shirt. Woman's got nice tits, for sure.

"Is there a reason you're sitting in Levi's chair like you own the damn place?" I demand, straight to the point. I smirk, knowing exactly why she's in here.

She swallows and lifts her chin. "He's asked me to stay here until he returns."

I arch a brow at her. "And if you don't?"

Her brows crash together. "He won't be pleased."

In another life—hell, a few months ago—I'd be into playing some games with Levi and Kristyn. And as much as watching Levi fucking Kristyn gets my dick hard, the idea of sweet Rowan pinned beneath me naked and squirming nearly maddens me with lust.

"You best be a good girl and obey him," I warn, my voice cold and authoritative.

She shifts in her chair, crossing her legs. "Yes, sir."

I chuckle as I leave her be. Levi lucked out finding that juicy, compliant little thing. So eager to please.

And while sir has a nice ring to it...I much prefer Daddy.

———

When I walk into the house through the garage, it's quiet. Brock and Hayden are gone. The younger boys should be at football. That means I have the house to myself for a while. I shed my jacket and throw it over a chair before bounding up the stairs. Since Brock's room has a direct view into Rowan's, I head straight there. As I'd hoped, I find her curtains wide open. The moment she sees me, she smiles and runs over to the window. Both windows are closed, so I can't hear what she's saying. Her mouth moves, and I think she says, "I missed you."

I point at her, then point to the ground in front of me.

She quickly looks over her shoulder, then back at me, a frown marring her pretty face. It doesn't take a rocket scientist to figure out she's trying to tell me her dad's home.

Gritting my teeth, I point in front of me again. "Now."

Her eyes widen at my word she could no doubt read. After a moment of hesitation, she holds up a palm and nods.

I stalk away without another glance. Trotting down the stairs, I ignore all the pictures on the wall—pictures Julia hung once upon a time. They're of the boys when they were smaller. I haven't updated them. I'm not sure I'd even know how to open the back and put the pictures in. So, they stay, frozen in time. The cunt left us and it's her loss. Those kids needed her, and she left. I may be a shitty parent, but at least I'm here. I teach them how to be real men and not think with their hearts.

Hearts are fucking ridiculous.

Real men think with their cocks.

The bigger the cock, the smarter they are.

I'm just stepping into the foyer when the front door opens. Rowan peeks her head in. She's done her makeup dramatically. It makes me want to scrub it all away. I like it when she looks pure and fresh-faced.

"Next time, no makeup," I say, my voice cool. "You're

beautiful, but you don't need that shit on your face. Save it for when you're an old lady."

She stalls in the entryway, red splotches blooming on her neck from embarrassment. Jesus, she's so easy to read.

"Come, angel."

At the nickname, her shoulders relax and she starts my way. She's gorgeous tonight in a pair of jean shorts and a black tank top. I love that her legs seem to glimmer under the chandelier. Soon, I'll have them wrapped around me.

"Kneel," I say in a soft voice.

She bites on her lip, hesitating only briefly, before she falls to her knees. I reach forward and stroke her hair. "I love how well you listen. It makes me want to reward you."

"I wore your necklace," she says with a shy smile. "I didn't take it off, even when I bathed."

I smile at her. "Then you do deserve a reward, angel." I hold my hands out to her. She takes them and allows me to pull her to her feet. I tug her to me and wrap my arms around her slight frame. Her entire body seems to melt against mine.

"You smell good, Eric."

"You smell better."

She giggles, and my cock hardens. Fuck, this is the best thing I've done in quite some time. Life can get boring when you get whatever the hell you want. She's something I've wanted for so long—since she was fifteen and I saw her doing cartwheels in my front yard. I promised myself right then I'd wait until she was ready for me and make her mine on her eighteenth birthday.

"Take off your clothes and leave them on the floor. They need to know Daddy is busy," I tell her and kiss the top of her head.

She looks up at me from beneath her dark, heavily painted lashes. "They hate me now."

"Does it matter what my sons think, or does it matter what I think?"

"You," she breathes.

"Correct. Now, take your clothes off. I hate asking twice."

She quickly peels off her tank and tosses it to the floor. Her black bra pushes her full tits together and up. As much as I love the look, I want to see her pink nipples. All it takes is a nod of encouragement and she frees her tits from the bra. My gaze is piercing as I watch her undo her jean shorts. They fall to the floor at her ankles, then her panties get pushed down too.

"Beautiful," I praise. "How's my pussy?"

She giggles, and my cock jumps in my slacks. "She's good. You kind of hurt her yesterday, but I soaked in the tub last night. Everything feels better now."

"Did you play with yourself?"

Her smile falls, and she shakes her head. "No. Was I supposed to?"

Such a sweet, innocent thing.

"No. Definitely not. You're not allowed to pleasure yourself. That's my job. Understood?"

"Of course."

I hold my hand out to her. "Come with me."

She grips my hand tightly. I love this kid's enthusiasm. Since she's been in my house a thousand times, she walks behind me, knowing exactly where we're going. My room. We enter my space that's long been redecorated to erase Julia from my presence. Dark greys and black furniture. It's my domain and one of the few places I can relax.

The only two women I've had in this room are Julia and now Rowan. I've fucked women in my pool and the guest rooms, and even my office. But none ever got to come to my room.

Rowan is a very special girl.

"How do you think this is going to go?" I ask as I point at my bed.

She walks over to it and sits on the edge. "Um, it'll hurt again?"

I chuckle as I tug at the knot of my tie. Her eyes are zeroed in on my movements. She's nervous, but trying so hard to be brave. Sweet girl.

"Your necklace looks so pretty on you. It makes me want to dress you in lots of jewelry." I toss the tie and start unbuttoning my shirt. "What would you like next, angel?"

She smiles innocently. "Maybe some earrings?"

"Of course. I'll find some as pretty as you."

Her lashes bat at her cheeks. She drinks in the compliments and praise as though it nourishes her sexy little body. *Drink up, angel. You're going to sweat it all out soon.*

I shed my shirt and drape it over an armchair, then take off my wife beater. Her hot gaze is on my chest like it was in the pool two days ago. I tug at my belt, and she winces.

"Your ass bruised?"

She nods. "It hurts to sit."

"You won't try to suck anyone's dick but mine now, will you?"

Her head shakes in vehemence. "No."

Letting my slacks fall to the floor, I kick out of them

and my shoes. I pull off my dress socks, because I'm not a fucking grandpa who fucks in socks like her precious daddy probably does. My dick strains in my boxers, and I grab at it.

"I'm going to fuck you gently, angel," I reveal, my voice soft.

Her eyes, I swear to fucking God, flicker with hearts in them. "Really?"

"First, I'm going to kiss that wet cunt. It's wet, is it not?"

"It's very wet," she breathes.

"Lie back and spread your legs," I order. "Did you get on the pill today?"

"I took my first one this afternoon," she tells me as she lies back. Her cunt is a pretty pink this evening, no longer abused like last night.

"In a month, I'll be able to come in you all the time." I prowl over to her and push my boxers down. My erection bounces out heavily. Most women go fucking bananas over my dick because older women love big cocks. I'm unsure how Rowan will take it, though. Her little cunt could barely take my fingers. She'll grow to love it eventually.

I kneel in front of the bed and inhale her scent. I love the smell of innocence. It makes me so fucking hungry. She whimpers when I grab her thighs and push them farther apart. Her pussy opens up to me like a flower. I want to go straight for her little bud and suck all of her nectar from her.

"Does Jax know you're here?" I ask before pressing a soft kiss to her clit.

She mewls and shakes her head.

"I need to hear you."

"No. I went out the back door. My radio is on, so he'll probably think I'm just taking a bath or something," she murmurs.

"What will he do when he finds out?"

"He won't find out," she assures me.

I run my tongue up her slit in a teasing manner, enjoying the way she whimpers. "Oh, angel, he'll find out.

Us daddies always know what our kids are up to. The question is, what will he do when he finds out?"

"I don't know."

Using my thumbs, I pull her outer lips apart and lick her harder than before. Her back arches off the bed. I love how sensitive she is. Her taste is so damn addictive. She whimpers and moans as I lose my mind a bit. I devour her sweet cunt until she cries out, her entire body shuddering. Pulling away, I admire the pretty girl on my bed. About damn time she's here.

"You taste so good," I praise. "I love your scent."

Her cheeks turn bright red. "I smell?"

"You smell like your body needs mine. It's a scent that speaks to my inner animal."

"Oh."

I stand, and my dick bobs in front of me. Her eyes drop to my cock, and she bites her bottom lip.

"Do you want me to suck it?" she asks.

"Not tonight, angel. Tonight is about you."

"Really?" Her surprise can't be masked. She's so

fucking cute. So easy to lure into my web of depravity.

"Really. Now, answer my question. What's going to happen when he finds out?"

"I think he's going to be mad," she says with a sigh, her eyes still on my cock.

I stroke it for her. "Of course he will. You're his little girl. I'm going to be defiling you. He'll be fucking livid."

Her brows scrunch together. "I'm scared. What if he...what if I can't see you anymore?"

At this, I laugh. "I could ruin your daddy in three days. Destroy all of his work. Burn his house to the ground. Take away everything he owns. I make a shit ton more money than he does, angel. He wouldn't dare."

"But..." She frowns, and her nose turns pink. "Please don't do that."

I walk over to my end table and retrieve a condom. After I rip off the wrapper, I roll it onto my dick, then walk back over to her. "I'll do whatever needs to be done to get what I want."

"He'll be mad, but let me talk to him. I know he trusts

me to make good decisions," she says, her chest heaving. I love watching her tits jiggle. One day soon, they'll be purple. My teeth marks will ruin her creamy flesh.

"I'm a terrible decision," I admit with a wolfish grin.

"No," she says adamantly. "I...like you."

"I like you too. Now, come here and let me kiss your pretty mouth."

She brightens and throws herself into my arms. Our naked bodies meld together with my hard cock pressed between us. I love the way her perky tits feel smashed against my firm chest. Her tits are real. Most of the women I've been with in the last few years have had fake tits. When they reach a certain age, they like to try to regain their youth. I don't mind fake tits, but these real tits are divine.

I grab her slender throat and squeeze hard enough to leave a bruise. I'm about to paint her neck with purples and blues so her daddy won't be able to ignore what I've done to her. Just as she starts to wheeze for air, I let up and attack her mouth with mine. The kiss is anything but sweet. It's a mating of two people about to join for the first time.

But unlike the other women I've been with, Rowan is a keeper. I knew it the day I saw her pink panties when she was doing cartwheels. Girls like her don't come around often. And when you find them, you have to snag them up and keep them.

She's mine, and Jax Wheeler can't do a goddamn thing about it.

SIX

R O W A N

HE DIZZIES ME. HIS MOUTH OVERPOWERS ME EASILY. Just like every other aspect of Eric Pearson's life, he dominates in the bedroom as well. I'm freaked out about how Daddy will react when he finds out I'm seeing Eric, but I can't find it in me to dwell on it. He'll be pissed, but I'm a grown woman.

"So beautiful," Eric murmurs against my mouth.

He tastes like me, and it's so weird, but I like it. His palm is tight around my neck, and the other one caresses my breasts in a reverent way. I love how he makes me feel cared for and adored. His fingertips brush along my necklace and a possessive growl rumbles from him.

"I need inside of you."

My heart thunders at his words. I nod and allow him

to guide me over to the bed. His arm wraps around my back as he lowers us onto the bed. It's all so romantic. I'm falling too hard and too fast for him. What happens when I go to college in the fall? Will we still see each other?

"Wrap your legs around me," he orders, his voice deep and demanding.

I obey, letting out a moan when his thick cock rubs against my clit. He's so much bigger than Brock. I'd been intimidated by Brock, wondering how he'd fit, but I'm almost terrified with Eric. He makes no moves to enter. Simply rubs against me in a slow, sensual way. His mouth sucks and bites on my throat until I'm clawing at his shoulders in need.

"Please..." I don't know what I'm begging for. I just need more connection.

He reaches between us and grips his dick. With soft whaps, he hits my clit with his dick. It drives me crazy with want. "Words. Tell me what you need."

"Make love to me," I breathe.

He chuckles, and it almost sounds dark. Like if you

told the devil a joke. Sinister and evil. It turns me on. "Tonight, we make love, angel." He kisses my mouth. "Tomorrow, I fuck you until you scream."

I whimper and dig my heels into his ass so I can lift my hips. I'm desperate to have him. He finally gives in and rubs the tip of his cock against my opening. It feels good. Then, he presses into me. Immediately, I stretch to accommodate him, and it hurts.

"Ow," I whimper.

"I know," he says softly. He's barely got the crown of his cock pushed into me and I'm afraid. When I lift my gaze to meet his, seeking assurance, I find his steely eyes burning a hole through me. "You must trust that I always know what's best for you," he says, his voice hard. With those words, his hand clamps down over my mouth. My eyes widen, but then he drives into me with a hard thrust that feels as though he's ripping me in two. The scream lodged in my throat fights for escape.

Pain.

Oh my God.

This hurts so bad!

He pulls almost all the way out, then drives into me slower. Everything burns and stings. Tears slip from the corners of my eyes. Once my body becomes acclimated to his intrusion, he removes his hand and replaces it with his mouth. I sob into his kiss, and he takes away the pain by distracting me with the hottest kiss known to man. I go from wanting to escape to clawing at his hair and pleading for him to go faster.

Our bodies, both slick with sweat, slap together. The sound is erotic, and I want to record it. I love it. His large palm grips my breast, and he pinches my nipple. It's like he's everywhere all at once. I can't keep up with all the sensations. He powers into me, and I'm unable to do anything but hold on for the ride.

His hand slides between us, then he's rubbing against my clit, like I can handle any more stimulation. It's too much, and my eyes water. I can't take all the assaults of pleasure.

"Too much," I cry out.

He ignores me and rubs faster, his hips thundering against me. When I'm about to lose my mind, I explode with another orgasm. It makes me clench around his giant cock, sending more waves of pleasure pulsating through me.

"Oh, Gooood!"

He grunts, thrusts harder, then exhales. His cock swells within me as his thrusting becomes uneven. All energy leaves him at once because he relaxes against me. His mouth peppers kisses all over my face, and I melt under his adoration.

My thoughts drift to Brock.

Brock was attentive, but he wasn't intense like this. There'd be no way sex with him would have even compared to the sex I just had with his father.

"Time to go home, angel. I don't want your daddy to worry."

He kisses me once more before pulling out. It makes me feel empty and used up. But then he flashes me a heated grin full of promise, filling all the holes inside my heart.

"I wish I could stay," I say with a pout.

He chuckles as he pulls off the condom. Even soft, his cock is intimidating. It drips with his orgasm, and I can't help but lick my lips.

"Next time he's away on business, you can stay over. I promise."

I stare at his toned ass as he saunters into the attached bathroom. I'm still stunned at the fact that I just slept with that man. I've lusted after him for years, but he was always a fantasy that would never come to be. He was way out of my league. But here I am, stretched and abused by his cock. It's incredible.

He returns carrying a wet cloth. In a sweet gesture, he kneels and wipes away my mess. It's such a tender and sweet move. I fall even harder for him. This is so bad. I'm going to fall in love with this man, I just know it. And for all I know, he just wants to have sex with a young woman. Eric isn't the type to ever bring the same woman around twice.

Once he's done, he deposits the cloth into a hamper, then finds some track pants. He pulls them up over his naked ass, but leaves his chest bare. I lick my lips.

"Don't look at me that way," he growls. "I promised you sweet, and I gave you sweet. If you keep staring at me like you want to suck me dry, we're going to be here all night and you won't be able to walk by morning."

I wince at that visual. My pussy hurts. If what he gave me just now was his version of gentle, I'm nervous about what he considers "fucking."

"Come," he orders.

I walk over to him and give him a shy smile.

"When you're in this house, nothing outside of making me happy matters. Understood?" he asks, his expression almost cold.

"Yes," I agree quickly.

"So, if I want to parade you through the house wearing nothing but my teeth marks, I will. No matter who sees. Do you understand?"

Shame courses through me. "They'll see me naked?"

"Perhaps," he says with a shrug. "But it doesn't matter. Don't worry about them. You're to only worry about me."

"Okay."

"Go dress." He narrows his eyes, challenging me to say no.

I swallow and lift my chin. "When will I see you again?"

"Tomorrow," he assures me.

"After work?"

"You'll know when I'm ready for you."

I'm slightly disappointed, but give him a nod. I walk past him, but he hooks an arm around my naked waist and pulls me to him. His mouth finds my ear as he gropes my breast. "I want you. Every second of every day. I will see you tomorrow without doubt, even if I have to walk over there and steal you from your father. Got it, angel?"

Relaxing against him, I nod. "Got it."

He lets me go and then disappears into the bathroom. Soon, I hear the shower turn on. With a sigh, I leave his bedroom. I don't see anyone, so I hurry to where I left my clothes in the middle of the foyer. I pick up my bra and struggle to put it on quickly. I manage to yank up my panties, only slightly wincing, then my shorts. I've barely got them fastened when I hear a voice.

"You fucked him." The words are cold and accusing.

Hayden.

"I don't answer to you," I bite out as I bend and snatch up my shirt.

He steps out from behind the staircase. His cheek is painted with four scabs from where I clawed him. I used to crush so hard on Hayden, but now he bothers me. It's like he's always creeping around me. If he'd have kissed me, then came for me the next day, we could have been a couple all along. He wasn't interested, though. It's like he's not into me unless someone else is.

"Nice bra," he mocks. "I bet Dad loves it. Did he put those hickeys all over you?"

I yank the tank top over my head. "Fuck you, Hayden."

He storms over to me, and I back up until I hit the wall behind me. I don't know what the hell his problem is, but he freaks me out. I'm about to kick him in the nuts when he gets pulled away. Rage, like I've never seen before, screws up Nixon's normally cool features. He hauls off and punches his brother.

With a roar, Hayden turns around and lays Nixon out with a powerful punch to the side of his head. Nixon crumples to the floor, completely knocked out.

"Nix!" I cry out, rushing over to him. He blinks at me in confusion. I turn my scathing glare to Hayden. "Get the hell away from us!"

He has the sense to look remorseful for hitting his brother. When the front door opens and Brock walks in, Hayden stomps up the stairs. Brock doesn't meet my eyes as he rushes over to his brother.

"What happened?" he demands, his voice sharp like his father's.

"Your brother is an asshole," I tell him.

Brock lifts his gaze to meet mine. I see sadness in his

eyes, but I am so done with him, it isn't even funny.

"Do you have this?" I ask.

He nods.

"Good. I'm out of here." I lean forward and kiss Nixon on the forehead. "Text me later and let me know when you're feeling better."

I get to my feet and run the whole way home without looking back.

SEVEN

E R I C

THE CONFERENCE CALL WITH OUR TAIWAN REPS lasted way too long. I thought I was going to nod off and pass the hell out. Last night, I laid in bed replaying everything that happened with Rowan. Her cunt was so tight. Best sex of my entire life. I'm addicted to her and can't hardly wait to have her again. Just thinking about her has my cock thickening in my slacks.

"Do you need any coffee while I'm up?" Kristyn asks, peeking her head in my door.

"I'm good." Normally, I'd be checking out her tits in her shirt, but my mind keeps flitting to a pair of the hottest tits I've ever had my hands on.

Kristyn leaves, and I get lost catching up on emails. I don't come out of the zone until I hear a knock on the door. Expecting Kristyn, I let out an exasperated huff.

"Hi," Rowan says from my doorway, looking drop dead gorgeous. She's wearing a peach-colored strapless dress that fits her body like a glove.

"Damn," I utter in appreciation. "What are you doing here, angel? I thought I made it clear I would come for you."

She pouts, but it doesn't deter her. "I missed you."

So needy.

I arch a brow when she closes the door behind her. Her fingers shake as she starts pulling at the zipper on the side. So fucking adorable.

"Did you come here to seduce me?" I ask, a hint of amusement in my tone.

"Is it working?" Her brows crash together as though she's worried I'll turn her away.

Fucking never.

"My dick is hard."

Her cheeks bloom rosy red. "Oh."

"Yeah," I say with a smirk. "Oh."

I pat my thigh. "Take that dress off and come sit in my lap."

She giggles and lets the material slide off her body. Her tits are bare, and her panties are a nude color. With her nude-colored heels matching her panties, she walks over to me looking good enough to eat.

"Tell me about your day," I murmur as she gets nearer.

Her tits jiggle as she awkwardly tries to sit in my lap. I yank her to me, and she relaxes in my hold. With my hands on her hips, I position her so she's straddling me, her barely clothed cunt rubbing against my eager dick. I lean forward and suck on her nipple until she squeals. When I pop off and grin at her, she playfully swats at me.

So fucking cute.

I love when she looks terrified, but I also love when adoration shines in her eyes. This girl is so desperate for attention. I guess her precious daddy doesn't give her enough. I reach up and tug at her necklace.

"Who do you belong to?" I arch a brow up at her.

She bites on her lip. "Daddy."

"Jax Wheeler?"

"You."

"Good girl. Tell me how your day was. Mine was fucking boring as shit."

She smiles as her hands tentatively touch my cheeks and ears. "I had school. It was boring too."

"Did you wear this to school?" A spike of jealousy, not a characteristic I'm used to, surges through me.

"Oh, no. I put this on for you."

I reach between us and rub at her clit through her panties. "You're so eager to please."

"I am," she agrees.

She squirms as I massage her. I love how wet her panties get almost immediately. Pushing them to the side, I enter her with my longest finger. Soaked. Always drenched, this girl. She rides my finger. Her motions are awkward and nervous. I let her spread those pretty wings and test out flying a little on her own. It's so beautiful to watch her find her sexuality.

"I need you," she whines.

I lean forward and suck on her tit. "I don't have condoms with me. You're going to have to come all over my fingers and then get creative as to how you'll get me off."

She moans when I push a second finger into her. Using my thumb, I circle her clit as I fingerfuck her.

"You could just pull out," she whispers.

And chance having more fucking kids? Screw that.

"Your cunt is too tight and juicy to pull out mid fuck. I wouldn't be able to, then I'd be at the drugstore buying you a morning after pill. Let's be responsible adults here," I chide.

Her lips purse out in a pout. She gives up on begging for what she can't have at the moment and loses herself to my touch. I bring her to orgasm quickly. A smug grin tugs at my lips the moment she throws her head back in ecstasy. Dark purple bruises mar her slender throat, and I fucking hope Jax got an eyeful. Something about that motherfucker rubs me the wrong way. I've hated his guts since the moment I met him. Like a living, breathing beast growing into an entity that cannot be contained. Taking his daughter from him sates my inner animal.

When she comes down from her high, I slide my fingers from inside her and hold them up between us. They glisten with her juices.

"Taste yourself," I order.

She frowns. "Why?"

A flare of anger surges through me. She must sense I don't like her asking questions because she grabs my wrist and pulls it to her mouth. Her fat lips, perfect for sucking cock, wrap around my two fingers. I groan when her little tongue darts out to taste herself. With my heated stare on hers, I push my fingers into her throat. She gags and tears well in her eyes. I pull my hand away and shake my head.

"Relax your throat if you ever have any hope of putting my dick there."

Her eyes drop in shame. Using my wet finger, I lift her chin until she's looking at me again.

"Don't ever hide from me," I tell her. "I'm trying to

teach you. Don't you want to please me?"

She nods. Her bottom lip starts to wobble and the sweet girl bursts into tears. I hug her to me and stroke her bare back.

"Angel," I croon. "I'm not mad at you. I'm simply stern. If I were mad, you'd know it."

"I'm sorry," she says, sobbing.

I chuckle and stroke her hair. "For what? Being so goddamned beautiful that I have a hard-on every time I see you?"

She lets out a breathy giggle and pulls away to look at me. "I want to do a good job. I want you to want me."

I slide my fingers into her gorgeous brown hair and pull her to me. "I already want you," I say with a grin before kissing the hell out of her.

She kisses me stiffly at first, but then her body grows heated once more. Her hips rock as she grinds against my dick in my slacks. God, she's such a temptation. I want to fuck her across my desk and make her scream. I'm about to suggest that, condoms be damned, when she breaks away and slides down onto the floor in front of my chair. Her hands are clumsy as she unbuckles my belt and pulls my hard-as-stone cock from my slacks. She furrows her brows in determination as she wraps her plump lips around the tip of my cock.

"Licking the tip is a tease," I say with a grunt.

She nods and attempts to take me further. Her nostrils flare as she focuses. I tangle my fingers in her hair and enjoy the way this teenager teaches herself how to suck dick. My office door clicks open and Levi opens his mouth to say something. His gaze quickly darts from the dress on the floor to me. When he starts to back out, I shake my head and point to the seat across from my desk.

He smirks and shrugs before sitting down. The file in his grip is forgotten as he stares at the back of the brown-haired girl as she sucks my cock. I drag my gaze from my friend. Rowan's slobber is running down my shaft. She's making a big fucking mess, but it's cute. Sometimes, when you're used to getting good head all the time, it's fun to get really bad head to switch things up a bit.

Rowan needs a lot of practice, and I'll let her practice any time she wants.

She tries to take me further, but gags again, more slobber soaking my slacks. Levi is amused as shit and grins wickedly at me. I know I'll owe his ass an explanation later. The sick bastard will want to know every dirty detail like a goddamn girl.

Rowan's hand gently touches my balls, and it throws me off my game for a minute. Her throat relaxes just a bit. It gives me the opening I'm looking for. Gripping her hair hard, I thrust up while bringing her head down, sliding all the way into her tight throat. It takes her a second before she freaks out, her throat constricting as she gags.

"That's it," I praise. "Relax your fucking throat."

A humming that sounds like a pained whimper buzzes up her throat, adding to the sensation, and I come with a groan. My seed spurts down her throat. She gags again, noisily, but thank fuck doesn't barf all over my slacks. Once I've emptied my orgasm into her little belly, I release her.

She jerks back and gags again. Her mascara runs down her cheeks, along with her tears. Snot and drool are smeared all over her face.

"You're quite a mess, angel," I chide as I grab a tissue from my desk and hand it to her.

She cries quietly as she cleans herself up. I grip her chin and smile at her, loving the way her brown eyes lighten.

"That was fucking perfect."

She smiles. "It was?" I love how raspy her voice is.

"So hot."

As she stands, I frown at her. "Remember how I said whenever you're with me, I'm the only thing that matters?"

Her body stiffens as she nods. "Yes."

Pointing past her, I alert her to the other person in the room. "Levi and I have a meeting. Don't mind him. I'll see you soon."

She makes a choking sound and shoots me a worried stare.

"Only me," I remind her, then slap away her hands now covering her tits. "Don't do that when you're around me."

She swallows and gives me another quick nod. With her eyes on the floor and hands at her sides, she walks around my desk and picks up her dress. She shimmies into it and zips the side.

"Rowan," I bark at her.

She jumps and turns my way.

"Don't I get a kiss goodbye?"

Relief flashes in her features and she all but runs to me. I let out a chuckle when she throws herself into my arms, her mouth attacking mine. I kiss her hard while gripping her thighs harder. She whimpers and squirms, but doesn't try too hard to get away. When we're both breathless, she pulls away.

"Go do your homework like a good girl."

She breaks away reluctantly, then starts for the door.

"Nice to meet you," Levi says with a wolfish grin.

A quick wave is all he gets before she bolts from the

room. Good girl. As soon as the door closes behind her, Levi chuckles.

"You found a good one I see," he says before tossing a file on my desk.

"I could say the same for you," I challenge. "Kristyn seemed awfully comfortable sitting at your desk yesterday."

His features darken. "She's a good one too."

EIGHT

R O W A N

I STARE IN THE MIRROR AS I STRAIGHTEN MY HAIR. ERIC said he'd come for me and I want to look perfect for him. I've dressed in a turquoise dress that bares my shoulders and creates a heart effect with my breasts. It's poufy and hangs about halfway down my thighs. I love it because it makes me feel girly. I'm just touching up my blood-red lip stain when the doorbell rings.

He's here.

My heart pounds in my chest as I slam the cap on the lip stain. I attempt to calm my nerves as I hurry down the stairs. Daddy texted earlier saying he won't be home until late, so I've got plenty of time to spend with Eric. When I open the front door, I suck in a sharp breath. Eric stands there with his hands behind his back, looking exquisite and expensive in his high-dollar, custom made suit.

"You look beautiful," he praises, his voice deep and gravelly.

I beam at his words, then bounce over to him. Throwing my arms around his neck, I kiss him as though I didn't just see him a couple hours ago. He chuckles against my lips.

"Aren't you going to invite me in?"

I pull away and frown. "You want to come in?"

"I want to see where my girl lives."

In all the years we've lived here, Eric has never been in my house. All four of his boys have, but not him. A thrill shoots through me. "Okay."

"But first," he murmurs as he reaches up and fingers my necklace, "I want to give you something."

I blink at him, my cheeks blushing with heat. "You do?"

"You deserve to be showered with gifts," he explains, his steel-blue eyes boring into mine.

When he holds out a jewelry box, I can't help but

squeak with excitement. I take it from him and find two shiny diamond stud earrings.

"Oh, Eric, they're breathtaking," I say in awe. They came from a jewelry store I don't recognize, but they look pricey.

He grins at me as he sets to putting each one in my ears. His hands are hot as they brush against the side of my neck. I'm desperate to have him. I clutch his hand and guide him into the house. He's quiet and patient as I show him each room. When I reach my dad's room, I intend to keep going, but he stops.

"There," he says, pointing into the room. "I'm going to fuck you there."

I stare at my dad's immaculate bed and shake my head. "W-What? No! Are you crazy?" I hiss.

Eric's jaw clenches and he glowers at me as though I've just struck him. "Excuse me?"

I bite on my bottom lip and stare helplessly at the giant bed. He'll know. If Eric fucks me there, my dad will know. I just have a feeling.

Eric looks at his watch before shooting me a cold stare. "Oh, look at the time. I need to go."

I'm shocked at his sudden mood change and panic rises inside me. "No," I breathe. "Please don't go." I reach forward and twist his tie around my hand as I plead with him using only my eyes.

He strokes my hair and shakes his head. "Why are you being so defiant?"

"I'm just worried." Tears threaten, but I keep them at bay.

"Why?"

"Because he'll know."

"And?"

"He'll be upset."

"You care, why?"

"Because he's my..." I trail off and frown. I feel like this is a trick. Eric's dark brow lifts in question.

"Say it. I know you want to," he says icily.

My lip wobbles. "He's my daddy."

He blinks at me, his jaw clenching. I'm worried this is

all about to end. A whimper claws its way up my throat.
"No, angel. Not anymore." Walking past me, he grabs one
of Daddy's pillows and places it in the middle of the bed.
"Straddle it."

I open my mouth to ask why, but then think better of
it. Eric doesn't seem pleased, and I don't want him to get
angry. Instead, I swallow down the humiliation of what
I'm about to do.

"Panties off before you climb onto that bed," he barks
out.

Reaching under my dress, I grab them and shimmy
them down my thighs. They fall to my ankles and I step
out. I climb onto the bed, then walk over to the pillow on
my knees. Once I turn around to face him, I straddle the
silk-covered pillow and wait for more instructions. His
grin is wolfish.

"Pull the front of your dress down. Let me see your
tits."

I nod, then release my breasts from the top. My
nipples are erect and desperate for his touch. Eric

unbuckles his belt, and I wince, thinking he'll spank me. Instead, he unzips his pants and frees his hard cock. He walks over to the edge of the bed and strokes himself lazily.

"Rock your hips. I want you to get off using that pillow," he says in a low voice.

"I don't think that's possible," I murmur.

His nostrils flare. "I think you like the belt on your ass."

"N-No!" I hiss. Without being told again, I start rubbing against the silky pillow—the same pillow my dad sleeps with each night. Shame burns through me. Once Eric leaves, I'll strip the case and wash it.

"Come taste my cock. You can do two things at once, right?"

I stick my tongue out at him and he chuckles. It lightens the mood. My pussy is wet, and I know I'm making a mess on the pillow. Bending forward, I position myself on my hands as I continue to seek what feels like impossible pleasure from a pillow. Eric guides his thickness past my lips, a satisfied groan escaping him the moment he pushes inside. His touch is gentle as he pets my hair. I close my eyes and relax. I love being the object of his affection.

He doesn't fuck my face like earlier in his office. Instead, he allows me to control the rhythm. I feel emboldened to take him deep. His hiss is all the encouragement I need. Bobbing up and down his length, I try to bring him as much pleasure as possible. My arousal soaks the pillow, but I'm no longer worried. I lose myself in the moment with Eric. Just when I think he's about to come, he pops out of my mouth and points at me.

"Lie on your back with your ass on the pillow. Spread your legs and show me what's mine." His firm command turns me on and I scramble to heed his instructions. On my back and fully exposed to him, I'm delighted when he crawls on his knees toward me. His thick cock bobs out in front of him. It's giant and beautiful. Soon, it'll be inside me.

He sucks on his two middle fingers, then pushes

them inside me. I love his fingers probing me. Today feels different, though. Like he has a different intention. I don't know what yet, but I trust him. He uses his other hand to rub my clit while he begins roughly fucking me with his two fingers. They're curled at an odd angle, and each time they thrust deep inside me, pleasure zaps through me.

"Pinch your nipples," he demands.

My palms jerk to my breasts, and I tweak the hardened flesh. So many sensations run through me, but the one I'm most focused on is deep in my core. Like something building within me. I whimper and try not to squirm. His finger on my clit moves quickly, and the ones inside me move so fast. So fast. I'm growing dizzy and overwhelmed with the need to explode. This feels different. I can't explain it, but I want it.

"That's it," he croons. "Let it go."

A sudden violent urge to pee makes me clench. "Oh no," I cry out in horror. I try to squeeze my thighs together, but he's too strong and doesn't let up. The sensation becomes too much to take. A wave of intense pleasure seems to make my entire pelvis contract. I think I'm having an orgasm, but it's so strange feeling. Heat. *Oh God.* I'm going to pee.

I gape down in absolute disgust as my body literally gushes. His entire hand gets soaked and it splatters everywhere. It runs down my crack, drenching the bed below me. He never lets up, and it's as though he's delighted I just peed all over him.

I burst into embarrassed tears when he jerks his hand from me. His eyes are manic as he regards me.

"I knew you'd be a squirter," he growls before pouncing on me.

His wet hand tangles in my clean, straight hair, and he rubs his dick against my messy pussy. Our mouths meet, and he kisses me hard. I've heard of squirting before, but never paid much attention to it. Now that I know I didn't pee on him, I relax. His cock feels good rubbing against me and I want it inside. When it slips and pushes into my soaked, still-contracting sex, he hisses out in pleasure. I love how fat his cock is. That he seems to split me in two. He slides back out and rubs it against my clit again.

"No, naughty girl. Do that again, and I'll whip your ass."

I frown and try to be good, but his rubbing becomes too intense. I find myself lifting my hips again, and he pushes deep into me again. I expect him to keep going, but he yanks away from me and climbs off the bed. He tucks his cock into his slacks and yanks off his belt.

"Show me your room," he bites out, his chest heaving. He's usually put together, but I love him like this. So shaken and wild. His shirt untucked and pants undone. His dark hair messy from me grabbing at it.

"Yes, Daddy," I say softly, hoping to cheer him up and change his mind.

His gaze darkens, and he flashes me a sinister smile. I slide my ass off the bed, leaving a wet trail in my wake. He crosses his arms over his chest, the belt hanging in a threatening way as he waits for me. I toss the pillow at the headboard and snatch my panties from the floor. The bed is rumpled, so I smooth it out. With a sigh, I reach up and turn on the fan, hoping it will dry things out before my dad gets home.

"This way," I whisper as I walk down the hallway to my room. As we near it, I hesitate. It's so girly and young looking. Suddenly, I'm worried he'll be turned off. When I stall, fire licks across the backs of my thighs, making me scream.

"I didn't say stop," he says lowly.

I run into my room, then turn around to face him. His brows are lifted as he slowly inspects the space—everything from the quilt with horses on it to the frilly valances above the windows.

"Hmmm," is all he says. When his eyes land on the dollhouse, he smirks. "That," he says, pointing. "I'm going to fuck you on that."

NINE ⎯⎯⎯⎯⎯

E R I C

SHE'S A PICTURE OF RUINED INNOCENCE. HER brown hair is messy and matted on one side. The mascara she'd perfectly applied is smeared from her outburst earlier. Bouncy as shit tits still hang out of the top of her sexy dress. But the best part? The best part is seeing her juices trickling down her thighs.

I'd thought it would take some work to get her to squirt, but in the end, I played her body like an instrument. She was a good little girl and came exactly as I wanted her to. All over Jax Wheeler's bed. The poor girl didn't know what happened to her. Probably thought she pissed herself or some shit.

Me, though?

I was proud as hell.

"Lift your dress and bend over. I still owe you a whipping."

She whines. "Please. I'll do anything. I don't want one."

I wrap the Italian leather around my fist and grip it tight. "Now, angel."

With a pout of her gorgeous lips, she obeys, lifting her frilly dress and baring her bruised ass to me. Purple and blue. Such pretty colors against her pale, creamy flesh. I run the belt between her thighs, and she trembles.

"Hold still now," I say before delivering the blows.

Whap! Whap! Whap! Whap! Whap!

She screams and stumbles forward, using the dollhouse as support to keep from falling. I don't wait for an invitation. Stalking her, I make my way over and fist her silky hair. With my other hand, I grab my cock and push it into her slick cunt. A loud moan rings out, making my cock twitch with delight. I thunder my hips against her, reveling in the slapping sounds of our flesh, knowing I'm hurting her ass more. She grips the top of the house to hold on as I pound into her from behind. As I drive deep, my knee digs into the dollhouse. I hear something cracking, and my knee pushes through. I pull back, then use the toe of my expensive shoe to shove into the house, gaining more leverage.

"Who's fucking you?" I snarl as I fuck her like a madman.

She cries out. "You!"

Releasing her hair, I slide my palm to her throat and clutch her hard. "That's not what I want to fucking hear, and you know it, angel!"

"D-Daddy!"

"Say it," I roar.

"Daddy is fucking me! Oh God!"

Her cunt squeezes my dick, because she's a dirty little girl who likes to talk nasty. My nuts seize up, and I come like a schoolboy virgin. Hot, violent, uncaring. She's unable to stop the way I pour my seed into her fertile cunt. The moment my dick stops twitching, I pull out of her, my cum dripping all over her white carpet.

She's so beautiful with her dress over her hips and body bent over her now destroyed dollhouse. Her ass is bright red, and she'll wear more bruises tomorrow. I'm just tucking my wet cock back into my slacks when I look out the window and see Brock gaping at me.

At least he knows who she belongs to. I wave to him before dropping the blinds. She manages to unfold herself from the dollhouse and sways on her feet.

"You look beautiful," I praise.

Her frown disappears as her eyes light up and she smiles back at me.

"We'll need to deal with our little accident in the morning, though. That wasn't very responsible, Rowan."

Chastised, she nods at me. "I'm sorry."

Chuckling, I motion for her to come to me. "Why? You're sorry your cunt is so fucking tempting I can't remember to wrap it up before screwing your brains out? Never be sorry for having such a perfect pussy, baby."

I hug her to me and kiss the top of her head. She kisses my neck and jawline, desperate for my affection. I pet my sweet girl and let her get what she needs from me. It's a two-way street, after all.

A beeping sound indicates someone just walked into the house. She jerks away and stares at me with terror in her eyes. So goddamn cute.

"My father," she chokes out, careful not to use the word daddy.

"I'll take care of this," I assure her. "Put yourself together. Quickly now."

She pulls her dress back over her breasts and swipes at her mascara. I brush my fingers through her hair while she straightens her dress. Never mind the fact that she has my cum running all the way down to her ankles.

"Do I look okay?" she asks.

I skim my gaze over her body. "Fucking perfect."

"Sweetheart," Jax hollers. "I got done early. I thought we could—" His words die in his throat the moment he reaches her doorway and sees me standing in her room.

"Whoa, killer. Wipe the murderous glare off your face. I was here to help Rowan. She called, absolutely in tears with fear."

His anger morphs into one of confusion. "What's wrong? What happened?"

"She thought there was an intruder," I tell him, the lie easily falling past my lips. "Turns out, it was a mouse. I almost got the bastard, but he got away." I gesture to the ruined dollhouse. "I tried to stomp on his ass, but it didn't quite go as planned."

His eyes remain glued to the dollhouse.

"If you need help carrying that thing out of here, I'll send over one of the boys. Rowan is a woman now. She doesn't need to be playing with dollies."

He snaps his head my way and bares his teeth at me. "Get the fuck out of my house, Pearson."

"Daddy!" she cries out.

We both snap at the same time, "What?!"

I burst out laughing at the way Jax's face turns purple. "Sorry, I have kids too." I shrug it off and push past him, clipping his shoulder along the way. It isn't until I'm home and catch my reflection in the hallway mirror that I see her red lipstick smeared all over the collar of my dress shirt.

I hope he fucking saw it too.

———

The next morning, I waltz into the high school and throw a nod toward the principal. I've donated so much fucking money to this school, nobody questions my presence. I walk into the office and snap my fingers at the secretary.

"Rowan Wheeler. I need to see her. Tell her Daddy is here."

The woman gapes at me in confusion, but doesn't ask questions. I hear her dial someone, then gives me a nod. "She'll be here soon."

I wait for a couple minutes, and soon, she walks in like a breath of fresh air. I inhale her sweet scent and flash her a smile. I'm happy to see she's wearing holey, stylish jeans rather than a dress. The shirt hanging off her shoulder makes me want to bite that flesh and mark her there so nobody steps near her.

"Eric?" she asks in confusion. "What are you doing here?"

I walk over to her and invade her space. The secretary is watching, so I don't do anything that will be gossiped about from now until the end of time.

"You forgot your medicine," I say as I produce a pill from my pocket. The morning after pill.

Her eyes widen in understanding. She holds out her palm, and I shake my head.

"I want to make sure you take it like a good little girl," I tell her.

The secretary makes a choked sound behind me. Okay, so maybe this shit will get gossiped about. Ignoring her, I focus on my girl. She opens her pouty mouth, and I press the pill on her tongue.

"Swallow."

She chokes it down, then gags.

"Open," I instruct.

The sassy girl rolls her eyes, and it makes my dick

hard. She'll pay for that later.

"Good girl," I growl. "Now, come give Daddy a hug."

She giggles and throws herself into my embrace. I squeeze her tight ass in her jeans, loving how she groans. The bruises must hurt. Burying my face into her hair, I seek out her earlobe with my teeth and bite on it.

"Something came up tonight," she says suddenly.

I pull away from her and glare at her. "What?"

She swallows and pouts again. "I have to hang out with him."

Reaching into my pocket, I pull out a pen. I grab her wrist and yank it to me. Quickly, I scribble my number onto her bare shoulder. She cries out in surprise.

"Call me when you can hang out with me." I flash her an icy smile that has her bottom lip jutting out.

I know she can't help that her father is an overbearing asshole, but she is eighteen. The girl could grow some balls and stand up to him. I won't push her, though. She'll have to learn that one on her own—just like she learned how to suck cock.

"Bye, Daddy," she breathes.

I wink at her before stalking out of the office.

"Is he really your dad?" The secretary asks her, but I don't wait to hear the answer.

———

"Cry me a fucking river," Levi says with a laugh.

I shake my tumbler that's now just ice and raise my glass to the cocktail waitress. She nods at me and scampers off. "Blow me," I snap, grabbing my dick for emphasis.

Levi grumbles. "I liked you better when you were single. You're more of an asshole when you're getting regular pussy from the same female."

I smirk and shrug my shoulders. "She keeps me busy."

"Why, because she's a damn teenager?" He lifts a brow. "Does her daddy pay you to babysit her?"

"He's not her daddy anymore," I say with a sinister smile.

"You're my motherfucking hero. Drinks are on me

tonight, buddy."

We spend the rest of the evening getting plastered. It's not like Rowan is coming over anyway. I should find one of these strippers and take her home with me. Get my dick wet for the night. But then, thoughts of Rowan's trembling bottom lip make it to the forefront of my mind. That girl has me all twisted up. Everyone pales in comparison.

"Hey, handsome," some busty blonde purrs as she climbs onto my lap. She's my normal type. Fake tits. Fake lips. Fake hair. But my dick doesn't speak porn star anymore. It speaks girl next door.

"Sorry, sugar, but the dick isn't interested," I tell her in a bland tone.

She seems to think this is a challenge and rubs at my cock through my slacks. It twitches for a second as I think about Rowan squirting all over Jax's bed. But as soon as it comes to mind, it disappears.

"I could make all your dreams come true," she whispers, lingering cigarette smoke clinging to her breath. "*Daddy.*"

Levi laughs, and I wonder if he told her to call me that to see if I'd bite. I'm not interested in anything this woman is serving. The daddy kink only works with Rowan. I'm not sure I'd even get hard over anyone else calling me that. With her, it just feels right.

"I'm not your daddy." I pull several hundred-dollar bills from my pocket and shove them into the blonde's panties. "Go take a smoke break."

Confused, she pulls away, gaping at the wad of money, then me. I wave her off.

"Bye," I bark.

Levi, who looks like he might pass out at any moment, shakes his head at me. "You're pussy whipped. By a girl who's still in high school."

"The pussy is the best I've ever had. Not in a hurry to go on the hunt for something different."

"Says every male before he runs off and proposes," he says with a roll of his eyes.

The thought of Rowan—cute as hell Rowan—

wearing my ring, sleeping in my bed, and her belly round with another one of my sons definitely has its appeal. I loved it when Julia was pregnant. Best sex we ever had in our marriage. Perhaps one day.

"You've lost your mind," he says in astonishment. "The great Eric Pearson is going to drive off into the sunset with his psycho neighbor's daughter. Never thought I'd live to see the day."

I pluck a cube of ice from my drink and fling it at him. "Keep talking mad shit and you won't live to see another day."

TEN

R O W A N

I'VE TEXTED ERIC A FEW TIMES, BUT HE HASN'T responded. I'm about to give up and go to sleep when I feel my phone vibrating.

"Hello?" I whisper, careful not to wake my dad. He never questioned me about Eric. I could tell he was pissed, but he didn't say a word. But then, he told me he was going to try to spend more time with me, so we caught a movie and had dinner tonight. All I could think about was Eric.

"Angel." His voice is raspy and vibrates straight to my core.

"I miss you," I blurt out.

He chuckles, and it warms me. "I want you in my bed."

"I want to be there."

"So get your pretty ass over here."

"Are you drunk?" I ask, stifling my giggle.

"Yes. Those strippers wanted my cock, but I saved it for you."

My jealousy is overshadowed by the fact that I've never heard Eric act like this. So out of control and not put together. "I'll be there in a minute," I promise.

We hang up, and I creep out of my bedroom. Luckily, Daddy sleeps heavily so he won't hear me slip out. I sneak downstairs and slip out the backdoor. Our alarm makes a beep, alerting us the door has been opened, but it never wakes my father. Once outside, I run through the grass across the yard. When I get to the Pearson's house, I'm happy to find the front door unlocked. Quietly, I slip inside and tiptoe to his room. A sliver of light pours from the cracked door.

I peek inside and stare at him for a moment. He's lost his shirt and lies flat on his back. His slacks are still on, but undone. All of his glorious abs are on full display. The trail of hair leading to his cock looks downright lickable. I push inside and close the door behind me. He lifts up on his elbows and regards me with a boyish grin I've never seen before. I'm almost knocked over by how much he looks like Hayden or Brock right now.

"There's my girl," he murmurs, his gaze raking down over the front of my nightgown.

I walk over to the bed and climb on. He guides my hips so I'm straddling him. His thumbs rub circles on my thighs just below the hem of my gown.

"You're drunk," I tell him.

He laughs. "And you're fucking cute."

"Just cute?" I sass.

He blinks at me, a lazy smile on his face. "Not just cute. Fucking adorable. Fucking gorgeous. Fucking mine."

I bite on my bottom lip. "That's better."

His expression is tender as he twists his finger around the end of my hair. I love him like this. Vulnerable and young. Carefree. When I lean forward to kiss him, he pushes me back. "I smell like smoke."

Rejection stutters my heart and I give him a fake smile. "Okay."

He strokes my hair. "Will you shower with me?"

His sweet question has me nodding. "Of course."

I climb off of him, then help him off the bed. He walks toward the bathroom, his steps slightly swaying. Once he gets the shower started, he undresses. His cock is hard and alert like always. I tug off my gown, then push down my panties.

"Come," he growls.

I take his offered hand and follow him into the spray of the water. As soon as we're under the heat of it, he clutches the sides of my neck with both hands and walks me backwards until my ass hits the cold stone. His kiss is deep and intense. With one kiss, he obliterates me. I wrap my arms around his neck, and he easily lifts me. Once my legs are hooked at his waist, he guides his cock inside me.

We're a perfect fit.

Kind of snug at first, but now we fit like we were made for each other.

He's surprisingly gentle as he fucks me sweet. I melt each time he kisses me. In true Eric fashion, though, he finds a way to hurt me. His teeth sink into my cheekbone, and he bites until I cry out, then chuckles as he kisses away the hurt. Because he's drunk, his efforts are clumsy, but I don't mind. I've been clumsy enough for the both of us this entire relationship. It's nice to see the perfect Eric Pearson falter and fuck up.

"I'm not going to be able to let you go," he murmurs as he grinds into me. "You'll want to go to college, but I won't let you leave me. I'm selfish. When I want something, I take it. If I want you, I'll take you."

His words turn me on. "You'll take me? Where?"

"Here. You'll be mine."

"I am yours," I breathe.

He groans as he comes suddenly. I don't get off, but I don't care. I love having him this way. His heat rushes into me once more. It feels better not having a barrier between us. Once he's done, he slides me off his dick, then starts soaping me down. His gestures are so sweet,

I can't hold in my smile. I take my turn washing him, and his intense stare bores into me. After we're clean, we rinse and dry off. Then, he carries me to bed. I feel like a princess.

He climbs in beside me and pulls the covers over us. I relax as he curls his strong, giant body around my small one. His palm gropes my breast while his nose nuzzles against my hair.

"I love you," I whisper.

"You've loved me since you did cartwheels at fifteen in my front yard. You liked showing off your panties," he says with a chuckle.

I smile. "So, you're not mad?"

"That you've always loved me?"

"Yeah."

"Not at all. Makes me want to fuck a baby into you and force my last name on you."

I shiver at his caveman words. "You like to tease me."

His palm slides to my hip, and he squeezes. "I'm serious as a fucking heart attack."

"You want to have a baby with me?"

"I also want in your ass."

I giggle. "You're bad."

He kisses my shoulder. "Go to sleep, angel."

"Okay, Daddy."

———

"Get up," Eric barks, dragging me from my slumber.

I roll over to see him standing beside the bed fully dressed for work. His dark hair is slicked back, and his face is freshly shaved. He's not wearing his jacket or tie yet. I can't help but stare at his muscled, veiny forearms on display since he's rolled the sleeves of his dress shirt up. He flips his wrist to check his watch.

"Jesus, Rowan," he grumbles. "I don't have time for this shit. I have a meeting this morning."

I sit up in bed and frown at him. Gone is the sweet man from last night who promised me the world. His cold demeanor is too much this morning.

"Open," he orders.

"What?"

He holds a pill up as an explanation.

"But last night you said—"

His glare is icy and cruel. "So help me, Rowan Wheeler. Don't make me shove this down your pretty little throat. I know you can take it." He smirks as though he's remembering how I choked on his cock.

I fight tears as I take the pill, all hopes of marrying him and carrying his child dashed in a moment. I slide past him and snatch up my gown he's laid out on the end of the bed. Before I make it to the door, he snags me by the elbow.

I wait for him to apologize or say something to comfort me. Instead, he kisses the top of my head and gives me a small swat to my ass.

"I'll come for you later."

I don't have the courage to tell him not to bother.

With emotion tearing at my throat for release, I slip from Eric's room and dart down the hallway. My tears are free to spill, and they do, blurring my way. I run smack into a hard chest. Strong hands grip my waist. When I jerk my head up, I find myself staring into Nixon's eyes. He may only be sixteen, but he's every bit a man these days. With his concerned stare on me and loving arms around me, I rest my head against his chest and cry.

He's tense, but doesn't say a word on the matter. His constant muttering under his breath calms me as usual and I relax against him. I've just burst from his father's room wearing nothing but a silky nightgown. Instead of judging me or asking questions I don't want to answer, he simply holds me. Once my sniffles have subsided, he pulls away to look at me.

"I'll walk you home."

I nod, and my lip wobbles as more tears threaten.

He gives me a sad smile before swiping my tears away with his thumbs. Then, he grabs my hand in his gentle grip and fiddles with his shiny pocket knife, a habit he's known for doing when he's agitated. The walk is short, and as we make it to the back door, I start to feel nervous. Daddy will see me sneaking inside and he's going to want to know where I've been. A shiver ripples through me.

Nixon's brows furrow. "Rowan—"

"I know," I whisper. "He's just...I feel so..."

He runs his fingers through his dark hair and I get a glimpse of the bruise on the side of his face. My heart clenches. "I just can't stand to see you hurting like this."

"I'll be fine," I lie.

He rolls his eyes, and I let out a giggle. "I get it, though."

My eyes widen as I gape at him. "W-What?"

"Dad has that way about him. He's magnetic and strong. People gravitate toward him, and once they're swept in his vortex, they can't pull away. I'd give anything to feel any sort of emotion from him." His gaze hardens, and he clenches his jaw. "I just wish you didn't get sucked in. You deserve someone better—someone who's going to treat you like you're everything in the world to them."

I know he's right. I should end things with Eric and move on. College will be here soon. There will be plenty of guys to meet and date. I don't have to settle for a man who's burning hot one moment and freezing cold the next.

Oh, but those scorching times...

My heart stills.

I need more than someone to play my body. I need more than the occasional nice word and sweet gift. I need more.

"Rowan?"

"Oh, shit!" I cry out. "Daddy's coming."

Before I can formulate a plan, Nixon draws me into his warm embrace, cradles my cheek with one palm, and presses his mouth to mine. The kiss is soft and sweet at first, but then, as though hungry, his tongue meets mine. His kiss is a promising one, and it reminds me so much of Eric. I let out a tiny moan. The hand resting at the small of my back slides to my ass and he squeezes me. I'm confused and slightly turned on.

"What the fuck?" Daddy snarls from behind me.

I pull away from Nixon and turn to see my father glaring at us with his hands fisted at either side. "I-I just w-wanted to see him b-before school," I chatter out, my lie obvious even to me.

Nixon hugs me from behind. "We're together." His lie is much smoother. Why is he lying for me?

"Go home, boy," Daddy snaps. "I'm tired of the Pearsons crawling around my house like fucking cockroaches."

Nixon lets the hateful words slide off him without so much as flinching. He kisses the top of my head before releasing me. "See you soon, babe."

Babe.

I bite back a smile.

Nixon is a good guy. I owe him big for this.

"In the house." My father's voice is icy. "You're grounded for a year."

I try not to laugh. He's just angry and overreacting. I hug my dad and inhale his comforting scent.

"I love you, Daddy."

He squeezes me. "I love you too, Rowan, but I'm serious about the Pearsons. I don't want you near any one of those little assholes." Then, under his breath, he adds, "Especially Eric."

My heart sinks. Despite our little show, I don't think Daddy is buying that I'm with Nixon even for a moment.

Well, too bad for him.

I'm not with Eric.

Eric can piss off.

ELEVEN ———————

E R I C

I DON'T FUCK UP OFTEN. HARDLY EVER IN FACT. BUT when I do, it's hard as hell to admit. This morning, though, I fucked up, and I can't stop thinking about how damn sad she looked. I thought I could sleep with her and move on. Keep things fun. Rowan wants more than a nice lay in bed. She wants everything.

Just like Julia.

My chest aches at the thought of *her*. Anytime memories of her bleed into my everyday life, I want to take a blade and cut them all out. It's not fair. It's not fair that I gave her a piece of me no one ever got, and she threw it all away. Her accusations were fucking ridiculous, but she spoke as though she had proof. The horror and utter heartbreak in her eyes still haunts me to this day.

The same goddamn look Rowan gave me this morning.

What if she leaves me too?

Instead of feeling angry or annoyed, I feel uneasy. Like I might puke my fucking guts up. Rowan is under my skin. She's been there for years. I've just finally scratched at that itch. Problem is, she's contagious. The pretty little thing is going to spread and spread until she infects every part of me. Including my heart. Especially my heart. Ultimately my heart.

"Who killed your puppy?" Levi questions from across the boardroom table.

I snap my attention to that smug motherfucker. He wears a smirk and is slightly disheveled. I know what he's been up to. Dirty bastard. "Camden is allergic to animals," I blurt out, no inflection in my tone. Then, I turn my attention to my best friend. "Trevor, I need a property. The cutest damn one you have."

"Do what now?" Trevor asks, a dark brow lifted in

question. He looks fucking ridiculous today in a shitty pair of flip flops and his four-thousand-dollar Armani suit. I want to thump him upside his hard head and order him to go buy some goddamn real shoes. Instead, I huff and pin him with a hard stare.

"I need a property. Now."

"You're a fucking riot," Levi says, snorting with laughter.

I offer him my middle finger, but my attention is on Trevor. "Please," I utter under my breath.

At my one word, Trevor sits up and starts thumbing through his phone. "What square footage? I'm assuming beachfront. Are hardwoods a must?"

Trevor is really weird about his properties, but I've never asked this man for a thing besides his brain. And that's probably why he's already on the hunt for, no doubt, the best home he can find me.

"It doesn't have to be big. Quaint. Newer with all the amenities. Fully furnished if possible." I rub at the tension forming on the back of my neck. "I need it now."

"A. Fucking. Riot." Levi's repeated words earn him the bird again.

"I think I saw Kristyn flirting with that new mail guy," I mutter.

Trevor and I both laugh when Levi jerks to his feet and stalks from the boardroom.

"Asshole," I grunt.

Trevor holds up his phone. "This one okay?"

I scroll through the pictures and give him a nod. "When can I get the keys?"

"Follow me to my office and it's yours."

And just like that, I'm the proud owner of the yellow bungalow on 22 Seaside Lane.

———

I wait in the parking lot of the high school in a shiny red convertible Mustang with the top down. I've long since lost my jacket and tie and have rolled my sleeves up to my elbows. She will have to forgive me. I come bearing gifts.

All the kids look the same. A blur of teenage acne, skinny jeans, and cell phones glued to hands. I pick out my own kids as they stroll to their cars. Camden even waves at me as he and Nixon follow after Brock. But it isn't until Rowan walks out of the building with a busty redhead that everything seems to sharpen. Her brown hair is straight down her back and she hugs her school books to her ample chest. The skirt she's wearing shows off her slender legs and I want to spend the evening marking them with my teeth. As though she can feel me checking her out, her chin lifts and our eyes meet. Instead of the embarrassed, flushed look she gives me, I get a bitchy glare.

I climb out of the car and whistle at her. "Get in the car, Rowan."

"Fuck you, Mr. Pearson," she yells back. She flips me off and continues walking with her friend. The redhead stares at me with bright eyes and crimson cheeks. She'll make some man happy with those dick-sucking lips. But there's only one pair of lips I want around my cock, and those lips belong to Rowan Wheeler.

"Little girl," I bellow. "Don't make me do this in front of everyone."

She stops and glowers at me. "Do what?"

"You know what." I lift a brow and flash her a smug grin.

Her eyes narrow before she lets out a huff and tosses her hair over her shoulder. Without another word, she walks off away from me. Her ass is delectable, and it belongs to me—not all the dickheads practically salivating after her. With a growl, I stalk after her. Her friend lets out a squeal when I near them. I hook an arm around Rowan's waist and pull her against me.

"You're a bad girl," I murmur against her hair near her ear.

She squirms and fights against me. Her books clatter to the concrete as she tries to get away. "Leave me alone!"

Several kids stare at me in confusion. They all know who I am. Everyone knows who I am. Which is why nobody does shit. I've just staked my claim in front of the entire school. Bending over, I fold her over my shoulder. She screams and hits my lower back with her fists.

"Stop it!" I roar, slapping her thigh below the hem of her skirt.

She cries out and kicks again, so I smack her again. "I hate you," she hisses, venom dripping from her words.

Ignoring her, I storm back over to the Mustang and toss her inside. Wisely, she doesn't try to escape. Instead, she crosses her arms over her plump tits and stares ahead, ignoring me altogether. I fall into the driver's seat and buckle her in before doing the same. Then, I peel out past the buses and nearly mow down another blob of teenagers who all look the same. It isn't until I'm out on the main road that I relax. Once I get her into bed, I'll calm her ass back down. I know just what she needs.

"I'm sorry."

She tenses in her seat. I reach over and pull her arm away from her chest. She doesn't protest when I thread her fingers with mine and pull our conjoined hands to rest on my thigh.

I don't give her any more words until we pull into the driveway of the yellow bungalow on Seaside Lane. As soon as I shut off the car, I let out a sigh. "I don't do feelings well," I admit, my voice low.

She turns her head and looks at me with curiosity beneath her thick lashes.

"In case you can't tell, I'm a guarded person," I deadpan.

Her giggles have me relaxing a bit more. "You don't say."

"You are so perfect. I want you so badly. It's too much for me to handle. My instinct is to shut down because I can't go down that road again." I frown as I regard her. "But the moment I convince myself I'm just fucking around with a hot-ass teenager, I want to laugh at myself. I'm not just fucking around. I like you too much. And not just for your tight little body but for your sweet smiles and laughter. I just enjoy being around you."

Her nose turns pink and she blinks away tears. "You hurt my feelings today."

A slice of pain rips at my chest. She's already inside me. I'll never get her out. Not that I want to. It just isn't happening, so I need to stop fighting it.

"I'm sorry, Ro."

She flashes me a brilliant smile. "Ro?"

"It's cute. Like you. Like your house." I wave at the bungalow.

Her dark brows pinch together. "My house?"

I climb out of the car and walk over to her side. When I open the door for her, she frowns as she stands. I grab her tiny waist and haul her against me. Her firm tits press against my chest. It works like magic to get my dick hard. I'll have her naked soon. Very soon.

"With the boys and your father, we can't have the time I'd like us to. Here, you can come after school and I'll meet you after work. When you're in college, you can live here instead of the dorms. We can spend time together in private." I feel like a pussy for even suggesting such shit, but the bright smile on her lips tells me it's exactly what she wants.

"You got us a house?" she asks in astonishment.

"And that car is yours too," I tell her with a smirk.

She slaps at my chest in a playful way. "No way!"

I slide my palms to her ass and kiss her forehead. "I'm sorry I acted like a dick, Rowan. I can't get enough of you. I know I'll fuck up some more, but don't be so quick to give up on me. It's not like you'll get away anyhow. I'll find you, angel. I'll always find you."

Scooping her into my arms, I revel in her youthful squeal. I tote her over to the house I spent the day stocking with necessities. Her lips press against my cheek when I carry her over the threshold.

"This is crazy," she says with a giggle. "What will I tell my father?"

I set her to her feet in the middle of the living room. "Tell him you got a job babysitting and it'll require some overnights and weekends."

She marvels at the nice home. It's not as fancy as either of our homes in town, but it's hard to beat the beach. The house is cute, just like I requested. Trevor didn't disappoint. I know it makes him mental to give me one of his many, many houses, but he'd do anything for me. I don't ask a lot of him and I'm happy he came through.

"Can I look around, or are we...?" she trails off and bites her lip.

"Oh, angel, we're going to fuck. I'm going to fuck you on every surface of this house. But for now, look around and get comfortable. I want you to feel at home here."

She throws her arms around my neck, then wraps her legs around my waist. Her lips attack mine as she playfully kisses me. This girl is the cutest damn thing I've ever seen. I chuckle against her mouth.

"I take it you like it?"

"I love it," she breathes. "Thank you."

"I really am sorry," I tell her softly.

She hugs me tighter. "I know. You're forgiven."

——TWELVE

R O W A N

THIS MAN DIZZIES ME.

Hours ago, I cursed the very ground he walked on. Now, I'm giggling and spinning around like a schoolgirl because he bought me a "fuck" house. I mean, that's essentially what it is, after all. But I don't even care. He's trying. He knows he messed up by being a jerk today and is trying to make up for it.

When I open the refrigerator, I let out a gasp to see it's fully stocked with food. He comes up behind me and presses his hard cock through his slacks against my ass. "Hungry?" His voice is husky and inviting.

"Yes," I murmur, rubbing my ass against him.

He slides his palm under my shirt and pinches my nipple through the lace of my bra. "I'm starved. I'll cook you something."

I let out an unladylike snort of surprise. "You're going to cook?"

He laughs as he grabs my hips and moves me to the side. "I always cook."

It's true. All the times I've been over with Brock or one of the other boys, Eric has been the one to cook. Mostly, he grills out and they eat a lot of salads. I grin stupidly at him as he sets to pulling steaks out. We spend the rest of the evening cooking, cleaning, and laughing. When Eric isn't so serious all the time, he's actually pretty funny. I've never seen him so relaxed. It gives me hope.

"I love the sound of the ocean," I tell him once we're settled on the couch in the dark living room. He's opened the sliding glass doors and the moonlight pours in, blanketing us in its light. The warm ocean breeze slides in and fills the space around us. Crashing waves in the distance are relaxing, and I can't help but yawn.

"Me too," he agrees, his fingers running absently along my back.

"This is nice. Being with you like this."

"You calm me," he says softly.

I tilt my head up to look at him. His normally styled hair is kind of messy from my constant touching and a lazy grin tugs at his lips. In this moment, he's carefree and young.

I make him this way.

My heart expands in my chest.

The hard, emotionless, powerful Eric Pearson is relaxed and happy in my presence. I'm no longer sleepy as my body begins to thrum with need. I pull away from him and stand beside the sofa. His hawk-like gaze is on mine, intense and focused. I love the way his eyes follow the movements of my hands as I slowly peel away my clothes. His cock strains against his slacks, and I'm desperate to have him inside me.

"What's your favorite part about me?" I purr, my palms roaming over my breasts.

He boldly rubs his cock through his pants and shrugs. "All of it. The whole package."

"You have to pick one thing," I tease.

He makes a motion for me to turn around. His large hands cup the curves of my ass. "This. It's so damn enticing. There are things I want to do to your ass you're not prepared for."

A shiver of want ripples through me. "Maybe I want them. You could prepare me."

He lets out a throaty chuckle that has me rubbing my thighs together. "Straddle my legs and put your hands on the coffee table."

I move across his legs stretched out in front of him and bend over. Everything feels open and exposed to him. When he runs his palms up the outside of my thighs, I let out a sigh. His lips press kisses to the inside of my thigh near my pussy, and I moan.

"I want this," he growls as he squeezes my ass cheeks and pulls them apart. His tongue slides along my slit to my asshole. I squirm against the foreign sensation.

"You want to lick it?" I ask in breathy astonishment.

With firm pressure, he pushes his tongue inside the

tight hole. It's wet and hot and burns a little, but it's also completely exhilarating. He slides it back out and slaps both my ass cheeks. "I want to fuck it, angel. I want to put my tongue in there first. And then, I'm going to finger your hole. I'm going to stretch it out so you can take my fat cock. What do you think about that?"

I groan at his words. My legs shake with need. "I want to see what it feels like."

His tongue pushes inside me again. Just as I'm growing acclimated to the sensation, he starts massaging my clit. I whimper and tremble. My tits jiggle as I find myself rocking against his tongue, forcing him to fuck my hole with it.

"Too much," I whine.

He ignores me and grips my hip with a strong hand. Pulling me to him, he dives his tongue deep inside. It's strange and kind of gross if I let myself think about it. As soon as I start pondering things like E. Coli, he pinches my clit, and I cry out, my knees buckling. He growls against my hole, and I lose it.

"Eric!" I scream his name as though it's the answer to all of life's questions. He doesn't let up until I'm coming down from my dizzying high.

The moment he eases his tongue out of me, he's barking orders. "Bedroom now. I want your pretty ass in the air. I'm taking it tonight."

I'm zoned out, still buzzing from my orgasm as I make my way to the room. He disappears into the bathroom for a few moments. The water runs as he brushes his teeth. When he emerges, he's completely naked. The only thing he wears is a feral grin and an evil glint in his eyes. He pounces on me, and I don't try to get away. I let him capture me because I love being in his strong arms with his thick dick slapping against my skin.

"It's going to hurt," he growls, no softness whatsoever in his tone. "A little girl like you wasn't meant to take a big cock in her ass." He slaps my butt cheek before reaching over to rummage in the drawer. I assume he's after a condom, but I hear the pop of a cap behind me. "But we're going to make you take it anyway, aren't we?"

I nod as he climbs on the bed behind me. I try to look at him over my shoulder, but can't see what he's doing anyway. Settling for staring out the dark window overlooking the beach, I fist the covers and push my ass toward him.

Slap!

I whine, but love how the spark of pain sends currents of pleasure straight to my core.

"You can't decide halfway through you don't want this," he says, his tone deadly. "That's fucked up, Rowan. Either we do this, or we don't. There is no middle ground."

"I want it," I breathe.

His lubricated cock slides along the crack of my ass, but doesn't enter me. I wiggle my butt at him, earning me a husky chuckle. God, he's so sexy. This man could do anything to me and I'd somehow find it erotic. I crave him like my next breath. I want him with everything in me.

"You're my boyfriend," I tell him boldly, as if I have

any power of negotiation over him.

His palm cracks across my fleshy bottom again. "No," he murmurs, his voice a gritted whisper. "Boyfriend is a title for a pussy. I'm your goddamn man."

With those words, he grips my hip with one hand and begins pushing into the tight hole of my ass. Where his tongue felt forbidden and exciting, this feels like an invasion. Fiery and painful and wrong.

I let out a scream as I yank at the covers, desperate to escape the pain. He doesn't go slow. Instead, he drives all the way into me, and an explosion of intense burning assaults me. My screams are silenced, though, when he reaches forward and wraps his hand around my throat.

"I know it hurts," he croons as he thrusts his hips against me. The slap of flesh is a hypnotic sound that distracts me. "But you'll learn to love it."

I choke as he brings me up off the bed and upright. He keeps one hand on my throat as the other roams to locate my clit. Tears stream down my cheeks, but all I can do is hang on for this excruciating ride. He rubs at my clit before sliding two fingers into my wet pussy. I groan at the sensation. I'm completely full of him. My ass throbs in pain, but my pussy is throbbing with need. His fingers fuck me hard, and the urge to pee overwhelms me once more.

"Eric," I sob. I want him to stop. I want him to never stop. My brain is confused. My body is responding even though I hurt. It doesn't make sense.

"Shhh," he breathes, his hips rocking against me. He nips at my shoulder, and my pussy clenches around his fingers. "Do you feel it?"

The building.

The fire inside me burning.

So intense.

"Y-Yes."

"You know what I want," he snarls. "Give it to me."

His hand works faster. He knows exactly where to touch me to make my body do things I never knew were possible. The intensity in my core becomes so out of control, I feel like I'm losing my mind.

And then, it happens.

Again.

A hot gush of an orgasm. Violent and messy. My scream is lodged in my throat as I soak us both. He's strong and holds me upright as he keeps the momentum of his hand inside me going, his hips never stop their thrusting.

I'm his.

I'm his to use, violate, and adore.

Rolling my eyes back, I give myself fully to him. I trust he won't let me go and allow his body to overpower mine in every way. My orgasm rolls into another one that sets off his. Heat floods inside me, burning my brutalized insides, but I love it.

"Mine," he breathes against the side of my neck, his body slowing to a stop. "All mine."

As he slides out of me and helps my weak body to the shower, I can't help but think how right he is. I was his all along. I was just waiting for him to come along and claim me.

Now that he has, I'll never let him go.

THIRTEEN———

E R I C

Two months later...

"YOU CAN'T TELL HIM," LEVI SAYS, ROLLING HIS eyes.

"Why not?"

"Because, hmm, I don't know..." he pins me with a glare, "he'll kill you."

At this, I snort. Jax Wheeler is a loser. Scum beneath my shoe. Some asshole who weaseled his way into my neighborhood. The only thing he ever did right in his life was spit some DNA into Rowan's mother's cunt.

"But can you imagine the look on his face?" I grin at him. Poor fuck would probably cry. Hell, he might try to beat my ass, but I don't spend hours every morning in the gym before the sun comes up just to let my dick of a neighbor kick my ass.

"I can imagine it," he says with a sigh. "I'm also pretty sure, deep down, he knows you're fucking his kid. All I'm saying is there's no need to provoke the beast."

"I'm the beast," I growl.

He shakes his head. "Whatever, man. We both know you're going to do what you want anyway."

Damn straight.

My phone buzzes from the table beside the pool lounger and I pick it up.

Angel: I'm on my way over.

Me: Hurry.

Angel: I miss you.

Smirking, I reply that I miss her too. And I do. The girl has crawled so far under my skin, I'll never get her out. At one time, I'd thought she was like Julia. Now, I realize she's better than Julia. Rowan is completely devoted to me. Julia wanted to be equals. I played her game for a while, especially when she was popping out my sons left and right, but I started to grow bored of it.

I like control.

I like to be the one in charge.

With my company. In my life. All aspects, I want to be on top.

My dick twitches at the thought of having Rowan beneath me last night. She whimpered and cried my name all night. The claw marks on my shoulder still hurt, and it makes me smile knowing she likes to mark me.

"You're so pussy whipped," Levi says as he stands and peels away his shirt.

I laugh. "And you're not?"

"Nope," he lies before running and doing a cannon bomb into the pool.

Me: Would you let Levi and I both fuck you at the same time?

I love getting her all fired up.

She doesn't respond right away, which means she's driving. When she finally reads her message, I can imagine her mouth popping open in shock and her cheeks blazing bright red. Cute as hell, my girl.

"Eric Pearson!"

Dragging my gaze from my phone to the back door, I find the source of the outraged screech. Holy fucking shit does she look like a goddamn dream today. She's wearing a pair of cutoff shorts that aren't buttoned or zipped and a tiny scrap of a white bikini top. It's just transparent enough I can see the dark outline of her nipples through the fabric. My cock responds by jumping in my swim trunks.

Levi curses in the pool, and I almost laugh out loud. Rowan is a temptation to every man in the vicinity. Doesn't matter if they're pussy whipped or married or anything. One look at her, and the vision goes straight to their spank bank for later. While they're fucking their pretty girlfriends or wives, they're thinking about my angel. Her succulent tits and cunt so tight, she strangles a cock.

I rise from my lounger and stalk over to her. I want her naked. I want her legs wrapped around me while

I bury my dick inside her. I want to fucking bite her. Having Levi here must have me feeling more possessive than normal because I'm three seconds from ripping off her clothes and marking my territory.

"My beautiful, sweet girl," I growl as I grab her by the hips and pull her against me. My cock is stone between us. I thrust slightly against her so she knows just what she does to me. Her palms go to my bare chest, and she smiles brightly up at me.

"My handsome boyfriend."

I chuckle and kiss her pouty mouth. She's just as possessive over me, which entertains me to no end. When we're together, she gets pissy if I even look in the same direction as another woman. Rowan Wheeler is territorial and jealous as shit. It turns me the fuck on.

"How much do you love me?" I tease.

Her smile falls, and she parts her lips. "So much."

I knew it. The girl was in love the first time I pushed my dick into her. "Good girl. Good girls make their men happy, don't they?"

She nods. "I want to make you happy."

I grab her wrist and kiss the top of her hand. "Good. Come with me." She follows behind me until we get to the steps of the pool. I wait for her to shimmy out of her shorts. This earns another curse from Levi. Once she's in her sexy, not-so-innocent bikini, I guide her into the pool behind me. I drag her until she's treading water. I love it when she's out of her safety zone.

"This needs to go," I tell her as I tug at the top of her bikini strings.

Her arms wrap around my neck, and she looks over her shoulder at Levi, her lip caught between her teeth.

"He's not going to touch," I assure her. "But he can watch. Watching is okay, right?"

"Yes. Is that what you want?"

"I want to show him what he can't have," I murmur as I pull her top away and let it fall to the bottom of the pool. Her tits jiggle with each breath she takes.

"I have someone. You know this," he utters from nearby. Close. Where he can get a good view.

"And you're not doing anything wrong," I tell him.

He grumbles out a *fuck you*, and I laugh.

"This needs to go too, angel," I murmur as I tug at the strings of Rowan's bottoms and throw them over at Levi. He catches them in one hand and doesn't let go. He backs away until his back is pressed against the side of the pool and stretches his arms out along the concrete ledge, relaxing.

I grab her hips and carry her over to him. "Levi, I need your help."

He arches a dark, challenging brow. "Maybe I don't want to help."

"Just give her a place to sit," I say with a cold stare.

His nostrils flare, but then he places his foot on the wall behind him, making a seat with his thigh. I set Rowan's naked ass on his leg. He looks uncomfortable, but I can see the gleam in his twisted eyes. The fucker is curious to see how far I'll take this.

She's mine.

The thought is fierce, and he must sense it because

he doesn't move a muscle aside from the one in his neck that keeps ticking.

"Don't let her fall," I instruct him.

With a reluctant grumble, Levi hooks a strong arm around her waist. Jealousy spikes through me. It's good, though. Seeing him with her in his grip is a good reminder of how much I want her. Her big brown eyes search mine. A healthy mix of curiosity, lust, and fear. She has her knees drawn together, so I push them away, making her straddle his hairy thigh. Her honey-kissed skin seems so fair against his tanned flesh. I reach forward to rub her clit between her hairless lips. She jolts at my touch and wiggles in his grip.

"Eric," she whines. Fuck, I love when she begs.

I push my fingers inside her. "Mmmm?"

"I don't want him. I want you."

"You have me," I tell her. "He's just watching."

"You're such a dick," Levi groans. His gaze is hot and angry.

"I know." I massage her until she moans, her orgasm

overtaking her. When she calms down, I twist her slight body around until she's facing Levi. I unfasten my shorts and let them fall to the bottom of the pool. "Hold her," I bark at him.

He groans, but stands up, pulling her naked flesh against his chest. She tries to look over at me, but I urge her to wrap her thighs around his waist. Before she can argue, I slide my dick into her slick pussy from behind. A loud moan escapes her.

"Tell her she's hot," I tell my friend, my gaze pinning him.

He clenches his jaw. "She knows she is."

"But she needs to hear it."

"You're hot," he bites out. His palms holding her upright slide ever so slightly to her ass, and my dick lurches inside her. I drive into her over and over.

"Eric," she moans.

He tilts his head up to the sky, baring his throat to me. If I were a dog, I'd tear it out. She's mine. He's touching her. And if I were a dog, I'd kill him for it.

But I'm not a dog.

I'm a man.

A man who controls this shit. Every single move. Every single breath.

Sliding my palm to her throat, I grip her until she hisses. Her hands go to his shoulders. Now that she's turning purple, my sick friend has no qualms at staring at my pretty girl. Her tits bounce against him as I grind into her. I release her throat.

"Tell Levi who I am," I mutter. "Tell him who loves you."

She shudders in my grip, her pussy growing slicker by the moment. "You do."

"Who am I?"

My girl knows the game.

"Daddy."

"Jesus Christ," Levi hisses. He's a kinky fuck like me.

"That's right," I snarl. "Say it louder so the whole goddamn neighborhood knows."

"Daddy loves me!" she yells, her body quaking with

pleasure.

The fucker loses control and bucks against her, his eyes wild with lust. He's clothed in just his swim trunks, but I can feel his cock pressing against my hand, desperately seeking her warmth. My hand slides to her tit. I revel in the sharp gasp of air that hisses from her when his cock rubs against her now that my hand is out of the way. I push and push and fucking push until I have them both pinned against the side of the pool. The water splashes around us. Levi grunts as though he's furious, and Rowan moans. When she cries out with her orgasm, I feel my nuts seize up in pleasure.

"Good girl," I grunt as I spill my seed into her. Levi makes a choked sound. The moment we all relax, he pushes her into my arms, then hoists himself out of the pool.

"Drinks later?" I call after him, enjoying a good taunt.

He lifts both hands in the air and flips me off before slipping inside the house.

"I guess we'll drink alone," I tease as I slide her off my

softening cock.

She twists in my arms and attacks my mouth with hers. "Did you mean it?" she asks breathlessly.

I grip her ass so hard, she yelps. "Of course I fucking meant it. I love you, angel. You're mine. What part of that needed clarification?"

She giggles. "All of it. Say it again."

I lean my forehead against hers. "I love you."

"I love you too, Daddy."

I fuck her again, alone, until she screams loud enough to let the entire neighborhood know what we're up to. Levi isn't the only one around here who gets off on that shit. She's mine, and I live to daddy the fuck out of her.

FOURTEEN———

R O W A N

THE WAVES CRASH JUST OUTSIDE MY OPEN WINDOW and I sigh. Graduation was last week. My father was proud, Nixon played the part of stand-in boyfriend, and my eyes never left Eric's as he sat in the audience. Each day, we somehow end up at my bungalow by the sea. When I can get him alone, I see parts of Eric nobody ever sees. Deep below the surface of the cool, composed businessman is something I'm desperate to know and love.

"I'm going to tell my father," I murmur, my voice barely heard over the gulls cawing nearby.

Eric, still half asleep, slides his palm over my naked ribs and mumbles. "Tell him what?"

He's lazy in the way he runs his thumb over my

nipple. As if we have all the time in the world to do just this. I wish it were true.

"That we're together. That I love you..."

His head is turned, his hair messy, but he finally looks over at me. He squints his eyes and dark hair dusts his cheeks. I love when he looks like this. So unkempt and unruly.

"There's not much he can do about it," he says, his full lips quirking up on one side.

He rolls onto his back while grabbing my hips. I'm easily pulled over to straddle him. His erection is hard and throbbing between the lips of my pussy.

"He might not pay for my college," I tell him as I rub against his length.

He groans and grips my thighs hard. "You never have to want for anything. You know I'll give you whatever you want, all you have to do is ask, angel."

His words turn me on. Gritty and feral. Possessive and protective. I grip his cock in my hand, then slide down over him. At one time, he stretched and hurt me.

Now, we seem to fit together painlessly and perfectly. Once I'm seated on him, I dig my fingernails into his pectoral muscles and stare into his icy blue eyes.

"I want to get married."

His hips buck into me and his glare becomes murderous. For a moment, I worry maybe I spoke the words too soon. But I can't help it. I saw how much my father loved my mother based on the pictures. Time is precious. The one you love could be gone in an instant. Wasting that time seems stupid. I don't want to waste another minute.

Plus...

I'm carrying his child.

We're a family now. We may as well make it official.

He rolls us over, then drives into me so hard, I cry out. His mouth attacks mine. Biting and sucking. He worships it with a soul stealing kiss. I run my fingers through his thick, dark hair and pray he'll love my body every day like this until we die.

He grabs hold of my thigh and pushes it up to the

point of pain. Eric loves making me open and vulnerable to him. From this position, he gets in so deep, I swear I can feel him in my stomach. I grow wetter for him with each passing second as my orgasm nears. Our bodies make obscene sounds as they slap together. His animalistic grunts have me moaning with need. He bucks his hips in such a way, he grinds against my clit each time. Harder and harder. Eventually, he pushes me right over the edge. I cry out and shudder beneath him. His groans carry on for a few more thrusts until he exhales loudly, his teeth moving to sink into my shoulder. My pussy clenches around his cock, setting him off. Heat bursts inside me. If I weren't already pregnant, I have a feeling he'd have just gotten me that way.

He doesn't pull out of me, even as his dick softens, and his orgasm trickles out of me. The bed is getting messy beneath me, but I don't even care. All I care about is having him every day.

"Why was she so special?" I ask, my tone bitter. The thought that he stayed with Julia long enough to have four kids annoys me. I don't like her. How could she leave him? He's beautiful and smart and successful. They had four kids together. If I ever see the bitch, she'll hear words from me.

"Julia?"

The fact that he knows who I'm talking about agitates me more. I blink back angry tears. "Yes."

He lets out a heavy sigh and lifts up to regard me. "She just got under my skin. I liked it. For the first time, someone had managed to do it. It completely fascinated me, and eventually, I grew to need that feeling."

I frown. "And me?"

"You're so far under my skin, I can't think straight." He presses a soft kiss to my mouth. "But I don't worry that you'll one day up and leave me."

"You worried with her?"

"Beneath the love for me and the boys, she always had suspicion in her eyes. I didn't have to cheat, because in her mind, I'd already done it. Nothing was ever good enough for her when it came to me." His fingers run through my hair and he stares at me as though I'm precious to him. My heart swells and I nearly burst into tears.

"She was a stupid woman to have left you," I tell him, my voice wobbling. "Especially since you had children together."

I'll never leave him.

Not now. Not ever.

"I've looked for her," he says, shame coating his words. I've never seen him look so lost.

I tense and swallow. "When?"

"Every day since the day she left."

Hot tears burn at my eyes, then spill down my temples. Suddenly, I want him away from me. I don't want him inside me. I try to push him off, but he's way too heavy. He must sense my mood change because he grabs my wrists and pins them to the bed. His cock starts to harden inside me.

"I hired a private investigator, Rowan. It's for the boys' sake. I didn't personally actively search for her each day. Someone is being paid to look." He leans his forehead against mine, and it only serves to make my heartrate skyrocket. "If I can find her, for them, I will. But I don't give a fuck if I ever see her face again."

"You still love her," I accuse, choking on a sob. I twist and attempt to escape his grasp. He pins both my wrists with his one strong hand and grips my jaw with his other, forcing me to look at him.

"No." His eyes blaze with fury. "Only you."

"Liar!" I yell, my newly out-of-control emotions raging.

He growls as he manhandles me onto my stomach. Once my face is pushed into the mattress, he settles between my thighs and presses his cock against the puckered hole of my ass.

"I never claimed her ass, angel," he hisses.

I scream at the top of my lungs when he enters me hard. I'll never get used to the way it feels. Like someone is trying to rip me in half with a hot poker. He doesn't slow or go easy on me. His fucking is brutal and claiming, like he wants to punish me.

I sob and squirm, but eventually give in to his feral ass fucking. I'm his. End of story. It's what he's telling me with his harsh thrusting and furious bites to my shoulder. Everything hurts, but the only thing I can feel is him. Eric. All over me. In me. He owns every nerve ending. My entire soul.

"There she is," he croons, his fucking slowing to a pace I love. Gentle and sweet. Caring. "My angel lost her shit for a minute, but she's back. My sweet, sweet girl."

I moan when he slides a hand beneath me to seek out my clit. The pain always gets shoved to the backseat when he pleasures me with his dick in my ass. It's weird how I go from hating every second to literally begging for more. I'm addicted to the brutality of it. The way he makes me feel entirely under his control.

My tears soak the sheets, but soon, it's my orgasm making the mess. With Eric, though, I never feel dirty. He always seems pleased when I let myself go. Our bodies mate so well together. It's like they've always known each other.

"Eric," I cry out as I become weak beneath him. All of my energy is gone. He continues rocking his hips against me, grinding his cock deeper and deeper into my ass, until he comes once more. I'll never grow tired of the way it feels to be filled with his cum.

"I don't know how many ways I have to spell it out for you, Rowan, but you're fucking mine," he breathes against my hair, his words furious. "Mine."

I nod, but can't get any words out. He slides his cock from my ass and settles his weight on me. His lips press against any bare flesh he can find. Sweet, yet claiming.

"I love you," he whispers against my shoulder blade. "Only you."

"I love you too."

"I know, angel. You only get upset because you care. It fucking moves me."

I smile and try to turn my head to look at him. He seeks out my mouth with his. His kiss is sweet and sexy.

"Next time you need a good ass fucking to remind you I love you, pretty girl, just open that sassy mouth and mention my sons' deadbeat mother." He chuckles as he kisses my cheek. "I dare you."

And as soon as my sore ass heals up, you can sure as hell bet I'm going to taunt him into proclaiming his love once more.

FIFTEEN————————

E R I C

One month later...

I MAY NOT BE A GOOD PARENT, BUT I'M AN EXCELLENT daddy to Rowan. She's been acting weird lately and texting someone. Once I spied and saw she was texting Nixon, I obtained the phone records from the cell company.

They're pretending.

It's kind of cute how he pretends to be her boyfriend so her father doesn't know who's really sticking his dick in her. But over the course of this fake relationship, I can see they've grown close. Nixon was always the kid I worried about, like maybe he has a few screws loose. Hayden is hard—jaded like Julia toward the end of our marriage. Brock is soft right now, but with the proper guidance, he'll end up the most like me. Camden is still young, but he has soulless eyes. They'll all go off to do well in their careers and in life. But Nixon? The kid is a thinker. His eyes always flickering with deep thoughts. Often, in a calculating, unnerving way. If the world were something he could slice open with his favorite pocket knife, he would. He'd dissect it piece by piece just to see how it all worked. He doesn't want to own said world or manipulate it like his three brothers. He simply wants to know why it is the way it is. I'd say perhaps he's the softest, but that's not true either. He's every bit as fierce as his brothers. Just different. Sometimes I wonder if Trevor is his real father.

We're headed to my house for a get together. I've invited Trevor, Mateo, Levi, and their women. My sons and their friends will be there. Several colleagues. Just some swimming and shooting the shit. I'm hoping Rowan will relax and come clean about what's bothering her.

"Everything okay?" I ask as we park inside my garage.

She sets her phone down in her lap, but her eyes won't meet mine. "I have to tell you something and I don't want you to get mad."

"As long as he doesn't touch what's mine, I don't care."

She flinches and glances over at me under her long lashes. "W-What?"

Narrowing my gaze at her, I reach over and pluck her phone from her hand. "Nixon."

"I wasn't talking about—"

"I know you're pretending to be his girlfriend for your father's sake," I tell her. "And as long as he doesn't kiss your pretty mouth or touch one hair on your perfect body, I don't care."

She wrenches the door open and hurries into the house. Her unusual behavior has me chasing after her. I'll find out what she's keeping from me. I toss her phone onto a table as I enter the house, stalking after her. She's barely made it through the kitchen when I hook her waist and yank her against me.

"What the hell is your problem?" I demand, my mouth pressed against her ear.

"We kissed."

Stunned, I freeze with her in my grip. "What the hell did you just say?"

She wriggles from my arms and backs away until her ass hits the counter beside the stove. "The day you were so cruel to me, Nixon walked me home. My father came out and we kissed so he wouldn't think—"

"What's with all the shouting?" a deep, challenging voice barks out behind me.

I swivel around to face my child. Sixteen and every bit as tall as me. Nixon glares at me with both his fists at his sides. His gaze flits over to Rowan as if to check on her. It infuriates me.

"You fucking kissed her?" I seethe, my jaw ticking with fury.

He snaps his eyes back to mine. No fear with this kid. He doesn't cower under my stare. I've perfected this hateful look. It's how I get what I want in business. And this kid doesn't even flinch.

"I did what I had to do," he snarls back.

"Eric," Rowan says behind me, her voice almost placating in nature.

"I'll do it again if I have to."

Rage overcomes me. I'm about to knock this kid into the wall when fucking Trevor waltzes in to save the day. All it takes is one look at me and he comes between me and my boy.

"Cool the fuck down, man," he urges.

"He fucking kissed my girl!" I roar, pointing at my son in a threatening manner. "I still own your scrawny ass for two more years. You even think about looking at her and I'll make your life a living hell."

"Enough!" Trevor roars, grabbing me by the shirt. "Cool your shit, asshole."

Nixon's nostrils flare behind Trevor as he stares me down. Fucking kid has balls of steel. He's still young enough, I could whip his ass and remind him who the man of this house is.

"Outside," Trevor orders Nixon. "Now, son."

I want to clock my best friend. It does nothing to assuage my suspicions. Of course, he'd never betray me, but I can't help but let my brain go there anyway.

Nixon doesn't move. "Rowan. Are you okay?"

She sniffles behind me. "Yeah."

"Because if you're not—"

"I'm fine," she says breathlessly. "Just go."

He lets out a frustrated huff, but storms off, slamming the door behind him. I may be pissed at him now, but he's the only one of my sons who ever had the spine to stand up to me. One day, when I'm not angry as fuck, I'll look back on this moment with pride.

"Cool your shit," Trevor says, his voice much calmer.

I give him a clipped nod. He smiles at Rowan, then strides off, his obnoxious flip flops slapping the marble floor as he leaves.

"It meant nothing," Rowan tells me, her voice firm. "You were a total asshole that day and your son stepped up to protect me. I didn't have it in me to deal with my father and he sensed that. You fucked up, and he fixed it."

I swivel around to find her glaring at me with tear-stained cheeks. She's so fucking beautiful, it makes my chest physically ache. Rowan Wheeler makes me feel things I've never felt before.

I'd kill for her.

The thought is sudden and blindsides me. But it's true. The love I have for her is a blazing inferno with no intention of being snuffed out.

"I did fuck up," I admit huskily.

She purses her lips and lifts her chin. I prowl over to her, expecting her to retreat. Instead, she relaxes the moment I have her in my arms. I kiss the top of her head and squeeze her hard.

"I'm sorry I'm such a prick."

She giggles. "You really are."

"I'm hard to love."

"To me, you're easy to love."

Her head tilts up so she can look at me. She slides her

palms to my scruffy cheek, her brown eyes lighting with adoration. It's expressions like these from her that seem to toss a match on my soul. I just fucking burn for her all the time.

"You deserve a romantic guy who will do sweet shit for you," I hiss as I capture her mouth with mine. I don't kiss her gently. I devour my angel. I inhale her essence. I suck all the goodness from her like the greedy fucker I am.

"I don't want anyone else. Just you."

I shove my hand into my pocket and pull out another one of her many gifts. I'd had a sweeter gesture in my head, but now seems like the right time. Grabbing her left wrist, I yank it to me and kiss the knuckle of her ring finger. When I slide the gigantic diamond on her tiny finger, she lets out a garbled sound.

It's huge.

I paid a fuck ton of money for it.

It costs more than her father's house. I made sure of it.

The ring means *mine.*

The inscription says *Daddy's girl.*

I don't know how much more forever it can get than that.

I'm not romantic, but I'll sure as fuck claim what belongs to me. And Rowan Wheeler will be a Pearson before the summer is over.

"Oh, Eric," she mutters. "When I told you and you never said anything back, I worried you didn't feel the same way."

I chuckle and kiss her pink nose. "No, it took that long to have this custom ring made. It came in this morning."

She beams at me. "Yes. The answer is yes."

I smirk at her. "I never asked, angel."

Her dark brows scrunch together in confusion. "But, I thought..."

"This ring means you're mine. I'm not asking. I'm telling."

A giggle escapes her. "Oh. You're such a caveman."

"If claiming you as my wife means I'm a caveman,

then so fucking be it."

"You should get on your knees," she says softly.

I want to roll my eyes at her, but if she needs me to ask on one knee, I will. Hell, I didn't even do that with Julia, but Rowan deserves a hell of a lot more than that bitch ever did. Lowering to my knee, I grab her hips and look up at her.

"Rowan—" I start, but she presses a finger to my lips to silence me. Then, her fingers grab the hem of her shirt, and she lifts, baring her stomach to me.

"Eric, I'm pregnant."

I stare at the slight pudginess. There isn't a baby bump by any means, but her tight, firm stomach has grown soft. After I got over my need to shove emergency contraceptive down her throat every morning, I embraced the idea of her carrying my child one day. With Julia, it felt like a trap—her way of keeping us together. Rowan, though, makes it feel natural. A strong, male urge to rise and beat my fists on my chest overcomes me. Instead of acting like a damn idiot, I press a kiss to her stomach below her belly button. Her fingers thread in my hair, and she lets out a ragged sigh.

"Are you happy?"

I inhale her soapy scent and kiss her flesh again. "So happy."

We stay locked in this moment for a bit. I can't seem to stop kissing her stomach. With the boys, I'd been filled with pride to have knocked Julia up with a part of me, but this feels different. This feels right. I'm more than happy. It means Rowan will always be mine.

Once I've kissed her until I'm sated, I stand and hug her to me. Arm in arm, we walk outside where the barbeque is underway. Brock and Hayden wear matching gloomy expressions when they see us. Nixon glares at me with a positively murderous expression on his face. And Camden is completely oblivious per usual as he shamelessly flirts with Mateo's date.

"You want to swim?" I ask.

She nods. "It's hot." Then her voice lowers. "It'll cool your baby off."

My dick responds in my trunks with a twitch. I watch with a wolfish grin as she peels away her clothes. Her bright yellow bikini is the perfect contrast against her skin, making her look even more golden and gorgeous. I give her ass a slap, loving the resounding squeal of outrage as she runs over to the pool.

"I think you successfully staked your claim," Mateo says with a chuckle as he hands me a beer.

I shrug and glance over at Trevor. His woman fusses over him, no doubt desperately trying to draw his attention away from the drop dead gorgeous teenager carrying my child. Levi is practically fucking Kristyn. She's sitting on his lap facing him and they're making out. If I had to bet money, he's the one hoping for a distraction. After our pool party of three, he's been slightly cold toward me and standoffish. He knows he fucked up and I now have leverage over him. It's good to have leverage over your friends in case they decide to try to screw you over one day.

"We're getting married," I blurt out as my attention

follows all four of my sons. Like planets being aligned, they seem to orbit around her, seeking her warmth and beauty. All four of them end up in the pool with her. Laughing. Flirting. Splashing. All four are probably hard as fuck over what's mine. Too bad they missed their chance. They'll learn. If you want something, you calculate your moves, then you play them—and you win.

I won.

Camden throws a football at me, and I toss it back before tearing off my shirt. I'm about to jump in and wrap my body around my woman so the boys will back the fuck off when I feel his presence.

Jax Fucking Wheeler.

"Rowan," he barks as he enters the yard through the open fence. "Time to go home. Now."

Everyone grows quiet, watching and waiting. Jax is the only one here who doesn't realize he's lost his little girl to the big bad wolf. He probably still thinks he can protect her from me. So sad for him, though. She doesn't want protecting. Rowan likes getting mauled.

"I just got here," she says with a pout, her arms crossing over her jiggly tits.

Nixon wades over to her in the water and wraps his arms around her from behind. I swear to fuck I see red. I should be filled with pride that he's trying to protect her, but I'm not. Especially when he boldly kisses her bare shoulder.

"Rowan," Jax growls.

"Out of the pool," I snap at the same time, my eyes pinning her in a fiery glare.

"Yes, Daddy," she murmurs. Like the good girl she is, she pulls away from Nixon and shoots him an apologetic look before taking the steps. With her suit clinging to her curvy ass, I'm about to nut in my pants. Fuck, she has a banging body. She grabs a towel and wraps it around her before coming to stand between us. He's inched himself into my yard, eyeing most of the males here warily, as if we're all going to gang up against him and beat his dumb ass.

The only one who wants to punch him in his stupid

face is me.

And maybe Trevor.

Trevor's glare is slightly crazed, and I wonder if I'm missing something. The annoying-ass chick he's been seeing since last summer, Lucy, tries to hide behind my best friend's giant frame. And, for once, it's not because of me. The bitch hates me and the feeling is mutual. This time, though, it has to do with Jax. One day, I'll ask him what that's about. Today, though, I have a statement to make.

"Jax," I say as I saunter over to him, a smug grin on my lips. "You should stay and join us. Rowan is always telling us how lonely you are. So sad, man."

Rowan shoots me a warning stare. Fuck her warning. I'm not afraid of her dickhead dad. And I'll be goddamned if I let her be afraid of him either.

"Rowan," Jax hisses. "I don't know what the hell you've gotten yourself into over here, but you're done with these assholes."

"Dad," she pleads, her voice quaking with emotion.

I stalk over to her and crowd her from behind. Over her head, I glare at her father. When I wrap my arm around her and kiss the top of her head, he gapes at me, completely and utterly frozen in shock. I splay my large hand over her stomach and grip her left wrist in my other.

"See this ring?" I say, my voice a low taunt. "It means she's mine now."

"The fuck you say?" His tone is deadly.

"Eric," she whimpers. "Not like this. Not here."

Ignoring her, I squeeze her tight and kiss the back of her hand, my piercing stare never leaving his. "She. Is. Mine." I curl her hand out toward him. The sun hits the massive diamond and glitters more light around us. "I put a ring on it."

"You fucking what?" he seethes, his face turning red with rage.

"I'm his fiancée," Rowan says primly, lifting her chin in a defiant manner. "And I'm pr..." she trails off when he takes a threatening step toward us.

"You will regret the day you laid eyes on her," Jax

whispers, his words violent, only loud enough for us to hear. The vein in his neck pulsates. "I will end you, Eric Pearson."

I flash him a brilliant grin and point to the gate. "Get the fuck off my property." I snap my fingers, then point to Nixon, who appeared out of fucking nowhere. "My son will show you out." I pin him with an evil glare. "Try any shit and I'll end you first."

Boldly, I grope Rowan's tit in front of her father.

"Tell him, angel," I murmur, my lips finding her ear. "Tell him how I already won."

She whimpers, but says the words he needs to hear. "I have a new daddy now."

"And her new daddy takes really good care of her," I rumble. "Really good care of her."

Jax's face becomes expressionless and he turns without another word. I watch with fucking glee as he storms out of my backyard.

"What did we just do?" Rowan asks.

"What we should have done a long time ago."

I pull her wet body into my arms and lift her. Her long legs wrap around my waist as she attacks my lips. All eyes are on us as I take her to the nearest location: the small pool shed. She cries out as I push her up against the shelves and tear her bikini bottom to the side to give me access to her greedy cunt. I manage to push my swim trunks down my thighs and grab hold of my aching dick. With a hard thrust that has her screaming for all to hear, I shove inside her and stake my claim. Again. And this time, I bet her old daddy can hear what her new daddy is doing to her.

I fuck her with the shed door open because I can.

I fuck her so loud, her screams hurt my ears.

I fuck her until I know I'll leave bruises on her.

She's mine, and I took her.

I'll take her again, and again, because I'm the motherfucking boss around here.

They all answer to me.

Even psycho-ass Jax Wheeler.

"Who loves you, angel?" I snarl as I nip at her lips and

chin.

"You!"

"Tell me what I want to hear."

She moans instead. I pull away and give her clit a slap with the back of my hand, my knuckles no doubt bruising her tender flesh. She cries out.

"Daddy! Daddy loves me!"

I laugh as I come deep inside her teenage cunt. It belongs only to me.

I laugh because every motherfucker knows it.

My boys. My friends. My neighbor. My girl.

And when my dick stops squirting out its seed, I lean my forehead against hers and kiss her plump lips. "I sure do, angel. I love you more than anything."

Except winning of course.

I laugh again.

ENJOYED THIS BOOK?
MEET THE OTHER FATHERS

Four Fathers Series by bestselling authors

J.D. Hollyfield, Dani René,

K Webster, and Ker Dukey

Four genres.

Four bestselling authors.

Four different stories.

Four weeks in April.

One intense, sexy,

thrilling ride from beginning to end!

These books were designed so you can read them out of order. However, they each interconnect and would be best enjoyed by reading them all!

She's not into him.
He doesn't care.

BLACKSTONE

A FOUR FATHERS STORY

J.D. HOLLYFIELD

OTHER BOOKS IN THE
FOUR FATHERS SERIES

BLACKSTONE
BY J.D. HOLLYFIELD

Contemporary Romance

I am meticulous. Structured. A single father.
I obsess over things and crave control.
And when a hot, feisty little woman throws a wrench in
my carefully laid out plans, I lose my mind.
My every thought revolves around making her bend to
my will—until they become less about her doing things
my way and more about just her.
My name is Trevor Blackstone.
I am an obsessive, complicated, demanding man.
People may not understand me, but it doesn't stop them
from wanting me.

KINGSTON

A FOUR FATHERS STORY

She works for him.
He doesn't care.

DANI RENÉ

OTHER BOOKS IN THE
FOUR FATHERS SERIES

KINGSTON
BY DANI RENÉ

Erotic Romance

I am arrogant. Insatiable. A single father.
I desire things that would make most people blush.
Normally, I find outlets that allow me to free the sexual
beast living within and play to my heart's content.
And when my voluptuous, innocent assistant starts
starving me after a little taste, I decide I'll let my inner
animal feed—on her.
Trouble is, once I have her, I can't let her go, and that
makes things complicated.
My name is Levi Kingston.
I am a dirty, ravenous, greedy man.
People may detest my kinks, but it doesn't stop them
from wanting me.

She's not his.
He doesn't care.

WHEELER
A FOUR FATHERS STORY

KER DUKEY

OTHER BOOKS IN THE
FOUR FATHERS SERIES

WHEELER
BY KER DUKEY

Dark Suspense

I am dark. Calculating. A single father.
I have secrets that would horrify most people.
Stalking is a habit I refuse to break—and what happens
after is a sweet reward.
My life is exactly the way I have designed it.
But an undeserving, sick monster is dating my only
daughter.
Until I deal with my problem, I can't truly enjoy
everything I've created.
My name is Jax Wheeler.
I'm a twisted, evil, insane man.
People may be afraid of me,
but it doesn't stop them from wanting me.

OTHER BOOKS

The Breaking the Rules Series:
Broken (Book 1)
Wrong (Book 2)
Scarred (Book 3)
Mistake (Book 4)
Crushed (Book 5 – a novella)

The Vegas Aces Series:
Rock Country (Book 1)
Rock Heart (Book 2)
Rock Bottom (Book 3)

The Becoming Her Series:
Becoming Lady Thomas (Book 1)
Becoming Countess Dumont (Book 2)
Becoming Mrs. Benedict (Book 3)

War & Peace Series:
This is War, Baby (Book 1) - BANNED (only sold on K
Webster's website)
This is Love, Baby (Book 2)
This Isn't Over, Baby (Book 3)
This Isn't You, Baby (Book 4)

This is Me, Baby (Book 5)
This Isn't Fair, Baby (Book 6)
This is the End, Baby (Book 7 – a novella)

2 Lovers Series:
Text 2 Lovers (Book 1)
Hate 2 Lovers (Book 2)
Thieves 2 Lovers (Book 3)

Alpha & Omega Duet:
Alpha & Omega (Book 1)
Omega & Love (Book 2)

Pretty Little Dolls Series:
Pretty Stolen Dolls (Book 1)
Pretty Lost Dolls (Book 2)
Pretty New Doll (Book 3)
Pretty Broken Dolls (Book 4)

The V Games Series:
Vlad (Book 1)

Taboo Treats:
Bad Bad Bad
Easton
Crybaby
Lawn Boys
Malfeasance

Carina Press Books:

Ex-Rated Attraction
Mr. Blakely

Standalone Novels:
Apartment 2B
Love and Law
Moth to a Flame
Erased
The Road Back to Us
Surviving Harley
Give Me Yesterday
Running Free
Dirty Ugly Toy
Zeke's Eden
Sweet Jayne
Untimely You
Mad Sea
Whispers and the Roars
Schooled by a Senior
B-Sides and Rarities
Blue Hill Blood by Elizabeth Gray
Notice
The Wild – BANNED (only sold on K Webster's website)
The Day She Cried
My Torin

ABOUT THE AUTHOR

K Webster is the USA Today bestselling author of over fifty romance books in many different genres including contemporary romance, historical romance, paranormal romance, dark romance, romantic suspense, taboo romance, and erotic romance. When not spending time with her hilarious and handsome husband and two adorable children, she's active on social media connecting with her readers.

Her other passions besides writing include reading and graphic design. K can always be found in front of her computer chasing her next idea and taking action. She looks forward to the day when she will see one of her titles on the big screen.

Join K Webster's newsletter to receive a couple of updates a month on new releases and exclusive content. To join, all you need to do is go to http://bit.ly/KWebsterNewsletter.

Facebook - www.facebook.com/authorkwebster

Blog - authorkwebster.wordpress.com

Twitter - twitter.com/KristiWebster

Email - kristi@authorkwebster.com

Goodreads - www.goodreads.com/user/show/10439773-kwebster

Instagram - instagram.com/kristiwebster

ACKNOWLEDGMENTS

Thank you to my husband. You're my rock. Always. I love you.

A big thank you to J.D. Hollyfield, Dani René, and Ker Dukey for wanting to take on this Four Fathers project with me. Without you all specifically, this was only a pipe dream. But because you three ladies are driven, work hard, are brilliant, and incredibly sweet, this was a fun undertaking. Perhaps we can do more in the future! Love you ladies!

A huge thank you to my Krazy for K Webster's Books reader group. You all are insanely supportive and I can't thank you enough.

A gigantic thank you to my betas who read this story. Elizabeth Clinton, Ella Stewart, Misty Walker, and Amanda Söderlund. You all helped make this story even better. Your feedback and early reading is important to this entire process and I can't thank you enough.

A giant thank you to Misty Walker for reading this story along the way and encouraging me! You're the most awesome friend a girl can have! I love you!

Thank you to Jillian Ruize and Gina Behrends for proofreading this book and being such supportive friends. You ladies rock and I adore you both!

A big thank you to my author friends who have given me your friendship and your support. You have no idea how much that means to me.

Thank you to all of my blogger friends both big and small that go above and beyond to always share my stuff. You all rock! #AllBlogsMatter

Monica Black, thank you SO much for editing this book. You're a rock star and I can't thank you enough for taking the time to make sure all four books flowed.

Thank you Dani René for formatting these books for us! You're amazing!

A big thanks to my PR gal, Nicole Blanchard. You are fabulous at what you do and keep me on track!

Lastly but certainly not least of all, thank you to all of the wonderful readers out there who are willing to hear my story and enjoy my characters like I do. It means the world to me!

Made in the USA
Columbia, SC
28 April 2018